SILENT GRAVES

SALLY RIGBY

TOP
DRAWER
PRESS

Edited by Emma Mitchell of @ Creating Perfection.

Cover Design by Stuart Bache of Books Covered

GET ANOTHER BOOK FOR FREE!

To instantly receive the free novella, **The Night Shift**, featuring Whitney when she was a Detective Sergeant, ten years ago, sign up for Sally Rigby's free author newsletter at www.sallyrigby.com

Chapter 1

'Morning, guv,' the sergeant on the front desk called out as Detective Chief Inspector Whitney Walker walked through the revolving doors into the spacious entrance lobby of the brand spanking new, state-of-the-art, ten-storey glass and concrete building which had been purpose-built for the Lenchester police force. It was situated on the edge of the city and had taken several years to complete. The building had been heralded as the best designed purpose-built station in the country. She'd reserve judgement on that.

Whitney and her team had only just moved in from their old Victorian station after a restructure and merger with Willsden, a force previously based thirty miles away. It had been a difficult time as each officer had to reapply for their positions. Whitney had lost some of her team and gained officers she'd never met before. Not only did she have a new building to navigate, she had a new team to build, too.

'Hi, Ted,' Whitney replied, flashing a smile in his direction, glad to see a familiar face from the old station.

'You're early.'

'You know me, I need a coffee before the day starts.' She grinned and hurried towards the ground-floor cafeteria, situated to the left of the large reception area. To the right, the wide corridor led to ten interview rooms, all with their own observation areas. No expense had been spared. In the basement was the custody suite and holding cells. On paper, it certainly beat what they'd had in the past. But where was the heart? It was cold and characterless.

After buying her coffee to go, she took the lift to the fifth floor and headed along the corridor to her new office, which she'd moved into over the weekend. It was square with a fancy, maple coloured adjustable desk that could be used both for sitting and standing. She also had a glass coffee table with four black low-level swivel chairs around it. Through the large, internal window she could see the incident room where her team would work. She closed the blind, so she wasn't visible and sat behind her desk with her hands wrapped around her cup. She was about to take a sip, when there was a knock at the door.

'Come in,' she called, biting back a moan.

The door opened, and Detective Constable Ellie Naylor stood there, her hands clenched by her side. What was wrong?

'Hello, guv.'

'Come in, Ellie.'

She hadn't expected anyone to be in at seven-thirty in the morning. She'd come in early to settle herself before everyone else arrived, in particular the 'new' officers, who she hadn't yet met. She thought it wise to have her caffeine fix first, as she didn't want to be cranky and get off on the wrong foot.

'Are you busy?'

'Not too busy to speak to you.' She placed her cup on the desk and gestured for Ellie to sit on a chair in front of her.

Ellie fidgeted before opening her mouth to speak. 'DCI Masters has sent me an email saying he's put in a request to have me moved to his team.'

'What?' Whitney spluttered. 'Under whose authority?'

The officer was the best researcher she'd come across in all her years on the force. She'd been placed on second-ment with Whitney's team three years ago, and they'd managed to keep her. It had taken all Whitney's persuasive powers and some, but she wasn't giving her up. Their impressive clear-up rate was, in no small part, due to Ellie's online expertise. What was extraordinary about Ellie was that she had no idea how good she really was.

'I think he was sounding me out as it wasn't a direct order.'

'Too right it wasn't. What did you say?'

Her fists clenched into tight balls. How dare he try to steal any member of her team without even speaking to her first? Not that it would have made any difference. She wouldn't give anyone over to that weasel.

'I haven't replied.'

'Good. Don't. Forward the email to me and I'll deal with it.' She paused. 'I'm assuming you do want to stay with me?' She'd better check, although she knew the answer.

'Yes, guv. I'd hate to go anywhere else.'

'Ditto. I can't do without you.'

The officer smiled. 'Thanks, guv.'

'You're welcome.'

Fortunately, after the merger, Whitney had retained her position, as DCI heading up a serious crime squad, as had

Ellie, Frank and Doug. But they did have two new people joining them. A sergeant to replace Matt, who'd moved to a smaller force with less pressure, so he could spend more time at home with his newborn baby, and a detective constable to replace Sue, who had moved to the West Mercia force.

Hopefully, the newly configured team could accommodate Dr Georgina Cavendish, a forensic psychologist who'd worked with them on several murder cases when the need arose. Whitney had no idea whether there'd be a budget for George to continue working with them, or if the new detective superintendent would terminate their relationship, but she'd soon find out.

She wouldn't let George go without a fight. She'd proved invaluable to their investigations in more ways than one. Not least because she'd been the one to locate Whitney's daughter, Tiffany, when she'd been kidnapped by a pair of psychotic twins intent on killing her. Whitney would be forever in her debt for that.

'What shall I do if he contacts me again?' Ellie asked.

'He won't. Not after I've spoken to him but if by chance he does, forward the email to me to deal with.'

'Thanks, guv.'

'Who else is in?' she asked.

'Just me.'

'I'll come through once everyone has arrived.'

'What are the new people like?' Ellie bit down on her bottom lip. 'Sorry, guv, I shouldn't have asked.'

Despite being with Whitney for three years, Ellie was sometimes reticent when talking to her.

'I don't know. I've yet to meet DS Chapman and DC Singh.'

'I'm so pleased Frank and Doug are still here, although I'll miss Sue and Matt. It will be strange without them.'

Matt had taken Ellie under his wing when she'd first arrived. They'd formed a tight bond, and he'd brought the young officer out of her shell. Whitney hoped the new sergeant would appreciate Ellie in the same way the rest of them did.

'I'm going to miss them too, but I'm sure the newbies will soon slot together. You go back and I'll come through shortly.' Whitney hoped she came across as reassuring, even though she was a little concerned about how they were all going to gel.

· 'Okay, guv.'

Ellie returned to the incident room and Whitney took a long drink of coffee, enjoying the warmth as it slid down her throat and the buzz she got when the caffeine kicked in.

On her desk was a list with the names of her team. The three she knew and the two she didn't. Her new sergeant was Brian Chapman, and the new detective constable was Meena Singh. Both of them had come from Willsden.

Would they fit in with the rest of the team? One bad apple could change their whole dynamic. But she wasn't going to think like that until she'd met them. It would be fine, she'd make sure of it. That was what leading a team was all about.

She also had a new boss as Jamieson had left for another position, which she certainly wasn't upset over. The new detective superintendent was Helen Clyde, who'd been on Whitney's interview panel.

It was early days, but from what Whitney had seen in the interview, the woman seemed to be straight up. It was the first time Whitney's immediate boss would be female, and she had no idea whether that was a good thing or not.

On the plus side, she wouldn't have to endure any of

the puffed-out chest, male superiority attitudes she'd had to suffer from so many of her superiors in the past, not counting Don Mason, who had long since retired, and who was the best boss she'd ever had. He was responsible for her career taking off as it had.

She glanced at her watch. It was almost time to meet the team. She opened her blind and could see they were all there. She sucked in a breath, and marched through, standing beside the new electronic whiteboard. She was all for new technology, but she'd also insisted on bringing with her their old faithful whiteboard, which she'd positioned next to the unused interactive one. She liked writing things down and sticking up photos. Okay, it could all be done electronically, but doing it the old-fashioned way helped her to think.

Did that mean she was getting old?

She turned to face her new team.

This room was much larger and far more spacious than her old one. There were desks with screens in the middle and at the opposite end of the room from where she stood they had a low meeting table with eight black swivel chairs around it, identical to those in her office. It was all very swish.

'Good morning, everyone, and welcome to the team. Now we've merged and have a new super, we're bound to attract the attention of the higher echelons.'

'I'd have had my hair cut if I'd known,' Frank said, as he patted his balding head.

'Which one,' Doug asked. 'There aren't many to choose from.'

'You can talk with—'

'Guys,' Whitney said, glaring at them and forcing her mouth to stay flat and not laugh. The banter between the two of them was legendary, but the new members of the team didn't know that. 'Can we at least give the impression to our new team members that we're a professional and hard-working set of officers?' She allowed herself a tiny grin. The pair of them often cracked her up with their *altercations*.

'Sorry, guv,' they both said, in unison.

'As we have some new faces here, I want you all to introduce yourselves. I'll start. I'm Detective Chief Inspector Whitney Walker. I don't want to be called ma'am. I'm not the queen. You call me *guv*. I've worked in Lenchester for the whole of my police career, and there isn't much about the place I don't know. What you see is what you get. I demand hard work and loyalty to the team and if you do that, we're going to get on very well.' She turned to the man sitting at a desk on her right. 'I'm assuming you're DS Chapman?'

'Yes, ma'am. I mean, guv.' He stood up. He was a tall, wiry man, in his late twenties, with dark blonde hair cut around his ears. He wore a dark suit, with a white shirt and patterned tie that was obviously expensive. The whole attire screamed he was going places. She doubted he would be happy staying as a sergeant for long.

'Tell us a bit about yourself.'

Many officers in her position wouldn't bother with the introductions, but for her it helped make the team cohesive which, in her experience, meant that cases had the potential for being solved far quicker.

'I'm Brian Chapman. I worked at Willsden for six months and before that I was at the Met where I trained.'

'The Met to Willsden. That's hardly a good career move,' Frank said.

Trust Frank to voice what, no doubt, they were all thinking.

'I moved for personal reasons,' Brian said, his voice flat.

'If you say so,' Frank quipped.

She was going to have to rein him in, especially as Brian was his superior officer. She was probably to blame for that as she encouraged her officers not to stand on ceremony with each other. And Matt, who had worked on the team as a DC before passing the Sergeants' exams, was just one of the boys when they were all together.

'Frank, show some respect. Not everybody wants to stay at the Met.'

'Sorry, guv. I was only joking. No hard feelings,' Frank said.

'Actually, I did want to stay, guv,' Chapman said. 'I had to go back to Willsden, my hometown, to take care of my mother. My father died several years ago, and she'd got to the stage where she couldn't cope on her own.'

Whitney glanced at Frank, who was looking decidedly sheepish, which she was glad about. His mouth ran away with him sometimes. This would give him pause for thought.

'I'm sorry to hear that,' she said.

'It's fine now. She's moved into a care facility.'

Whitney could relate to that, as her own mother was in care. She'd needed twenty-four-seven supervision when her dementia worsened. Guilt that she wasn't able to take care of her mum herself still plagued Whitney. Or care for her older brother, who had irreparable brain damage and was also in a care home.

'Are you looking to move back to the Met, now your mother's settled?' Frank asked.

The question on Whitney's lips, but not one she could ask in front of everyone.

'I haven't yet decided. For the moment I'm happy to be

here at Lenchester, which is recognised as a top force and, in particular, this is an excellent team.'

'Thank you, Brian. DC Singh, your turn,' Whitney said, looking at the other unfamiliar face.

The officer stood. Another one taller than Whitney. But then again, most people were, as she was only five feet four inches. The officer had dark hair, pulled back into a pony-tail, and a fringe. She was in her early forties, a few years older than Whitney.

'Hello, everyone. I'm Meena Singh and I was at Willsden for fifteen years. I met my husband there. We were both serving officers. Me in CID and him in uniform.'

Whitney had worked with husband and wife teams in the past. At least they weren't working together here, as those pairings were seldom successful. 'Did your husband come over to Lenchester as well?'

'No, he decided against it and has gone to work for a security firm.'

That pleased her as it meant no issues would be brought to work if there were problems at home.

'Frank, your turn,' Whitney said, turning to the older detective.

'I'm DC Frank Taylor,' he said, not bothering to stand. 'I've been here for more years than I care to remember and let me tell you, the guv's great. We're lucky to have her.'

'Thank you, Frank,' Whitney said, smiling.

'I've got another couple of years before I'm due to retire,' Frank added.

'How did you manage to keep your job in the restruc-ture, if you're nearing the end of your time?' Brian asked, arching an eyebrow.

Whitney stared at him. It wasn't an appropriate question to be asking, especially as he didn't appear to be saying it in a light-hearted way. Getting Frank back for what he'd said before? She hoped not. She didn't want antagonism in her team.

'Because I'm good at what I do,' Frank replied, laughing.

At least the older officer hadn't taken it as an insult.

'You are, Frank. But I'm more inclined to think you bribed the interview panel,' Doug said.

'You've probably already worked out that Frank and Doug have a *special* relationship,' Whitney said, looking at Brian and Meena, and shaking her head in fun. 'You'll get used to it. Doug, your turn.'

'I'm DC Doug Baines and originally come from Leamington Spa. I've been working with the guv for the past five years. She operates a tight team and I'm lucky to be part of it.'

'Thank you, Doug. Finally, over to you, Ellie.'

'I'm DC Ellie Naylor. I've been on the guv's team for three years. I echo what Frank and Doug have said about feeling lucky to be here.

'I'll interrupt here,' Whitney said. 'Ellie is our IT whizz, and what she doesn't know about technology isn't worth knowing. She's especially good at joining the dots where no one else sees them.'

'I'll second that,' Frank said.

'Me, too.' Doug added.

'I'd like to sit down and compare notes,' Brian said. 'Technology is my thing, too.'

'Um … okay,' Ellie said.

Whitney glanced at her new sergeant. Was he trying to muscle in on Ellie's territory? Assisting was one thing … taking over another. She'd keep an eye on things and make sure it didn't happen.

'Now that you've all introduced yourselves, we will—' The door opening interrupted her.

In walked the new detective superintendent. Helen Clyde.

Chapter 2

'Good morning, team,' Detective Superintendent Helen Clyde said as she looked first at Whitney and then to the rest of them. 'Welcome to the newly formed Lenchester CID. I'm sure I will get to know you all in time. Do you have any questions?' She looked around, but no one said anything. For once, even Frank kept quiet. 'I'm sure if you do, DCI Walker will answer them for you.' She turned to Whitney. 'We have a case. Let's discuss it in your office.'

Whitney frowned. Surely the new super wasn't going to be dishing out cases for them. It would be way below her pay grade. They'd come directly to Whitney before, as was procedure.

'Yes, ma'am.'

The team was quiet as she walked behind Clyde and they made their way to Whitney's office. The super was tall, maybe even taller than George. She was in her late forties, and had short, sleek dark hair, which she'd tucked neatly behind her ears.

Had the super come up through the fast track? Whitney would definitely be enquiring. Not that she was going to let that interfere with their relationship, although she had no patience for people who hadn't worked their way up through the force like she had. Her previous boss, Jamieson, was fast tracked and his knowledge of police work was slim, to say the least. But he had now gone after being appointed as Head of Intelligence Analysis for the South Wales Police. She had enjoyed his leaving party, in more ways than one. George had advised against her giving him a police manual as a leaving present when she'd suggested it.

'Please take a seat,' Whitney said as they entered her office. She gestured to the coffee table so they couldn't be seen by the rest of the team.

'Whitney, it's good to meet with you again. Is there anything you would like to ask me before I tell you about this case?' Clyde asked once they were both seated.

'Yes, ma'am. Are you planning to be distributing all the cases we take on or is it just this one?'

She had to get it out in the open, or it would be playing on her mind all day.

'Definitely not,' Clyde said, laughing. 'You don't need me breathing down your neck all the time.'

Whitney exhaled the breath that she'd been holding for what seemed like ages. Thank goodness for that.

'No, ma'am.'

'It just so happened I was there when this one came in and as I wanted to meet you and the team together to introduce myself, I said I would pass it on.'

'That makes sense, ma'am. I did think it a bit strange. What's the case?'

'Five days ago, skeletal remains from two bodies were found on a building site at Oak Tree Farm. Part of the farm had been designated for housing development, and the bodies were found after they'd started digging. The building work has now been suspended while the investigation takes place.'

'I know the farm, ma'am. It's five miles north of Lenchester.'

She also remembered that all hell had broken out in the community when the council had given permission for the development, because of what it would do to the countryside. There were petitions galore, but none were successful.

'You come from around here, don't you, Whitney?'

'Yes, ma'am.'

'I remember in your interview we spoke about you not wanting to progress up the ladder and that you were happy to remain a DCI. Is that still the case?'

Not *this* conversation again. Not everyone wanted to hit the dizzy heights of superintendent and above.

'That's correct.'

'I see. Did you ever consider working at another force, bearing in mind this is the only one you've experienced?' Clyde tilted her head to one side.

'I have personal reasons for wanting to remain in Lenchester.' Maybe once they got to know each other better she'd explain more fully, but for now this would have to suffice.

The super nodded. 'I understand. We're lucky to have you here, in that case. Other forces would have snapped you up in an instant should you have applied to any of them.'

Whitney allowed herself a smile. It appeared she was going to get on very well with her new boss. That should make her life much easier and would certainly put them on a more even keel. George would be happy about that.

'Thank you. I appreciate you telling me that.'

'I think you're going to like the new squad we've put

together, there are a lot of useful skills in there which you can utilise.'

'Yes, ma'am. I'm pleased to have three of my old members, and I'm sure the others will slot in well. I also wanted to ask you about Dr Cavendish, the forensic psychologist we've worked with before. Do you have any objections to the relationship continuing? I've always had a budget put aside for her.'

'I'm all for having a multidisciplinary approach, so continue using the doctor when you need to.'

'Thank you, ma'am. I'll go to the site and take DS Chapman.'

'Report back to me once you're done there. I want to know, as soon as possible, how long the bodies have been there, as we need to be mindful of the resource implications of investigating deaths from many years ago.'

Whitney's heart sank. Clyde had given the impression she wanted to keep her distance, but this sounded like she wanted constant updates on every step of the investigation.

'Yes, ma'am.'

'I like to operate in a fairly hands-off manner, but I do expect to be kept informed of major developments.'

That wasn't the impression she was giving. Whitney had initially thought it was going to work out well between them, now she wasn't so sure. It would be a case of *wait and see*.

'Yes, ma'am, I understand.'

'This is going to be the start of a very successful and effective team, I'm absolutely sure of it.'

The super opened the door leading out into the corridor which saved her from walking through the incident room. Whitney watched her striding away. It would work well, providing Clyde left her alone. She had no desire to butt heads, yet again, with her superior officer.

She returned to the incident room and stood next to the board.

'Listen up, everyone, we've got our first case. Skeletal remains from two bodies have been found at Oak Tree Farm.'

She wrote up the name of the farm on the board behind her.

'Isn't that the building site for all those new homes?' Doug asked.

'The place where they're going to build two hundred little boxes,' Frank added.

'It's part of Lenchester's development plan. We've no idea how long the bodies have been there, although it will have been for some time as they're reduced to bones. Brian, you and I are going to visit the scene,' Whitney said.

'Yes, ma'am.'

'Guv,' both Frank and Doug called out at the same time.

'Sorry, I mean, guv.'

'You'll get used to it. Ellie, I want you to start researching the development. See if there were any issues during the planning application process, I know there was a huge amount of opposition at the time, which was unsuccessful.'

'Will do, guv,' Ellie said.

'Frank, you can look into the farm, and its owners. See if there's anything useful there. Doug and Meena, you two look at missing persons cases, in particular those concerning two people. We're going to need to identify the bodies as soon as we can.'

'Yes, guv,' Doug said.

'Brian, what car do you drive?'

'A Volkswagen Golf,' he replied.

'New, or old and crappy?' she enquired.

'It's two years old, guv,' he said, frowning.

That suited her.

'In that case, you can drive. I'm sure it's a lot more comfortable than my old Ford Focus. I'll direct you to the site as I'm assuming you don't know where Oak Tree Farm is.'

'No, guv. But my satnav will find it.'

Of course it would. Why hadn't she thought of that?

She retrieved her jacket and bag and they left the room.

'What do you think of the new station?' she asked as they headed down the corridor towards the lift.

'It's much more comfortable than Willsden, which was run-down. The designers have done a good job.'

'We've got all the latest equipment, which is allegedly going to help us in our interviews, although I'm going to need someone to show me how to use it.'

Did she sound like a dinosaur? Probably. She wasn't, apart from where technology was concerned. There she had a blind spot.

'It's easy, you'll soon get the hang of it,' Brian said, his voice a tad on the patronising side.

'Good. Glad to hear it,' Whitney replied, ignoring his tone. 'Let's go and see about these two bodies.'

Chapter 3

'Take a left up here.' Whitney pointed to the track leading to Oak Tree Farm.

'That's not the direction the satnav is showing, guv,' Brian said.

'It's a shortcut locals know of. Trust me, it will take a good few minutes off our journey.'

'Okay, providing I don't get my car too dirty.'

Not another person precious over his car. He was as bad as George. She glanced out of the window. It was a typical December morning, cold, windy and with a damp mist in the air. The car wasn't going to stay clean, whichever route they took.

'I'm sure you can run it through the car wash if you do.' Though if he was anything like George, he'd wash it by hand in case it got scratched. She'd never understand people who loved their cars that much.

He turned and drove down the track, encountering potholes every few yards. Through the wing mirror, she saw dirt splashing up the sides of his ultra clean car. She wouldn't tell him. He could find out for himself.

'Where is it?' Brian said after they'd been driving a couple of miles, an impatient tone in his voice.

'Not much further and we'll be there,' she said to reassure him, despite not being sure. It was a shortcut she knew, but it had been years since she'd taken it.

'Okay,' he muttered.

They continued driving, and she breathed a sigh of relief when eventually a large piece of flattened land, surrounded by a police cordon, came into view.

Two yellow diggers stood on the track beside the blocked off area and Brian parked in front of them.

'Mind where you walk, it's very boggy,' she said, getting out of the car and stepping onto the mud.

She glanced down at her black work boots, which were already caked in mud, as were her trouser legs. She should have brought her wellies with her, but they were in the boot of her car.

They ducked under the cordon and made their way to a large hole surrounded by bollards, which presumably was where the bodies had been found.

'It's strange that someone buried the bodies in the middle of an open field,' Brian said.

'It hasn't always been like this. I'm fairly certain there were trees and bushes dividing the different fields, before all this land was cleared for the development. The farmer will confirm that when we speak to him.'

'So, this is going to be a housing estate,' Brian said as he scanned the place.

'Yes, unfortunately. People complained, but it fell on deaf ears as the county has a housing shortage. Perish the thought we get in the way of progress,' she said, grimacing.

'I don't see anything wrong with having housing developments rather than empty fields. It makes perfect sense to me,' Brian said.

'You're clearly not from the country, then,' she said.

In theory, nor was she, but her parents had often taken her away from the city when she was young, and she'd made a point of doing the same with Tiffany. It gave her an appreciation of an alternative way of life.

'No, I've always lived in a city. The closest I got to a farm was on a school trip, when I was eight. I got bitten by a so-called tame goat and that was it for me.'

Whitney bit back a smile at the image.

'You'll find people around here like the city, but also like having the countryside on their doorstep so they can enjoy it. I'm not going to get into a conversation about the legitimacy of the development, though, as it's a contentious issue and we probably won't agree.'

'No, guv,' Brian said.

She headed over to the hole from which the bodies had been taken, the mud squishing each time she placed her foot on the ground.

'There's not a lot here to see, apart from the digger's track marks,' she said, walking carefully around the perimeter. 'All we've got are two holes in the ground. Let's go to the farmhouse and have a chat with the farmer. He might be able to give us some more information.'

'Agreed, guv. Hardly worth getting so dirty over.' He grimaced and Whitney glanced at the state of his shoes and trousers. Did he regret wearing such expensive clothes to work?

They retraced their steps back to the car and drove to the large stone farmhouse, which was a further hundred yards down the track. It was three storeys tall and had a large open barn to the left of it, which was used as a garage, judging by the number of cars in there. She knocked on the racing-green wooden door and waited. She was about to try again, when it was opened by a man in his early fifties, with unruly, curly grey hair, and a deep lined forehead.

'I'm Detective Chief Inspector Walker and this is Detective Sergeant Chapman. Do you own the farm?'

'Yes, I'm Anthony Gibson.'

'We'd like to talk to you about the human remains found on your land.'

'I assumed they were human, after seeing them, but nobody would confirm when I asked. People have been here for days digging up my land. Finally, they left yesterday afternoon.'

'A forensic dig to recover remains properly isn't a quick job. There are protocols which have to be followed, and samples taken. They would have examined a wider area than where the actual bodies were buried, looking for forensic evidence and more remains.'

'I understand all that, but I need someone in charge to give me permission to resume the building work. Is that you? I asked the person who seemed to be leading the dig, but he said it wasn't for them to decide. We're on a tight deadline and can't afford to get behind. Losing five days is bad enough, any more could be disastrous.'

She scrutinised his face. Did he have no compassion? People had died on his land, and even if it was *hundreds* of years ago, he should show some respect.

'No work can be undertaken at present as this is a crime scene,' she said, coolly.

'How can it be a crime scene when people have walked all over it for God knows how many years? I'm assuming it's years as there were only bones found.'

'We'll let you know as soon as you're allowed to start work again, in the meantime we'd like to talk to you,' she said, as a gust of icy wind whistled around them and she pulled her coat tightly around her.

'Come inside,' he said, opening the door fully. 'We'll go through to the kitchen down the hall. The Aga's on so it's warm in there.'

They left their muddy footwear outside, beside the front door, and followed him through the hall into a farm-house kitchen with a flagstone floor. At one end was an Aga, next to a conventional oven and hob. In the middle stood a large eight-seater oak table. He gestured for them to take a seat.

'Would you like a coffee or tea?'

'Coffee would be lovely, thanks.' Whitney loosened her coat as the heat from the Aga warmed her.

'Same for me,' Brian said.

Whitney nodded her approval. Matt had always refused drinks for some reason. After placing the filled cups on the table, Mr Gibson sat opposite them.

'How many of you live here?' Whitney asked.

'Five. Me and my wife, who's visiting a friend in London today. Our fifteen-year-old twin boys, who are at school, and my father who moved back in here a few years ago after my mother died.'

'How long have you been here?'

'The farm has been in the family for over one hundred and fifty years. I grew up here and after going to agricul-tural college went to work in Dorset. I moved back with my family to one of the farm cottages twenty years ago, to help run the farm. My father handed over the reins ten years ago, and we moved into the farmhouse. He moved into one of the cottages with my mother.'

'What can you tell us about the housing development?' Whitney took a notebook and pen from her pocket. Although she had some knowledge, it was always better to get it from the source and not the reports in the media, which were bound to have been exaggerated.

'We're building two hundred houses on the land, a mix of two, three, and four-bedroom properties. There'll be houses to suit all budgets. We're also planning to build a grocery shop, a takeaway, and a small community centre. It'll be a sought-after place to live.'

'What made you decide to use the land for development, rather than continuing farming it?' Whitney asked.

'Financial reasons. The farm hasn't been doing well recently, what with the reduction in subsidies and the erratic weather we've been having. The upkeep costs are astronomical, far higher than most people realise, and the fields weren't being used. So, after much deliberation and discussions with the family, I went into partnership with a local developer. We still have a thousand acres left to farm to the east.' He pointed out through the kitchen window to an area in the distance.

'What sort of farming do you do?'

'Mainly arable, although we do have some cows and we also have a free-range egg production outlet, which my wife runs. It doesn't bring in a huge amount of money, and she mainly sells to small independent outlets.'

'Don't you mind having all these new houses being so close to you?' she asked.

'Once the development is finished, we will be planting trees and hedges to separate it from the rest of the farm. We won't be able to see them from our windows and they won't be able to see us. Why?'

'I'm just trying to get a picture of the development, as it will help with our enquiry.'

'Could you go into more detail about you needing money? Are you in debt?' Brian asked.

Whitney narrowed her eyes, tossing a glare in his direction, then realised he didn't know the golden rule: she did the talking in interviews. She'd forgotten to mention it to him as she was so used to being with Matt and he knew how she operated. He'll know for next time.

'You misunderstood. We weren't heading for bankruptcy, but the money from the development is going to be a useful backstop,' Mr Gibson said.

She'd love to be in the position of having a *backstop*, but that wasn't going to happen on a DCI's salary, especially with her outgoings.

'How are you funding the development before you sell the houses, if money is tight?' Brian continued.

She acknowledged that was an excellent question and one she hadn't thought to ask.

'We've already sold sixty-five per cent of the properties off the plan. It was part of the bank's requirements before they would grant us a mortgage. Also, we have a commitment from the local housing association for their statutory percentage. I'm not sure why our financial arrangements are relevant,' Gibson said, frowning.

'That's for us to decide,' Brian said.

'Let's move on,' Whitney interrupted. She wasn't going to have him upsetting the farmer, they required his cooperation. 'You obviously know the area where the remains were discovered. Can you tell me exactly what happened?'

'Yes. Wayne, the digger driver, had uprooted the hedges and cleared them away. He then began reshaping the soil and came across the bones. He stopped digging and ran over to the house to fetch me to take a look at what he'd dug up. After taking a look, and seeing the skull, I immediately phoned the police.'

'Do you have any idea who the bodies might be?'

'None whatsoever.'

'Do you remember anyone going missing in the past?'

He was silent for a few seconds and slowly shook his head. 'No. Sorry.'

'The actual place they were found ...
before the land was cleared for developmen

'The development goes across severa
bodies were found close to where there w:
of hedges.'

'Do you have a plan of the previous layout we can take
away with us so we can identify exactly where the bodies
were found and what the land looked like at the time they
were buried?'

'Yes. I have one in my office, I'll get it for you.'

He left the room, and Brian turned to her, his eyes
narrow. 'Why did you interrupt me when I was asking
Gibson about his financials?'

'I omitted to mention my rule to you, I ask the questions and you listen. I expect you to observe their reactions
and let me know what you've noticed. I'm not saying I
don't want you to ask questions at all, but I take the lead. I
also felt you were pushing Mr Gibson unnecessarily.'

'Why do you have this *rule*?'

'Because that's how I've always worked.' There was no
need to justify herself to him. He should do as she asked.

'What if you don't ask a question I think is relevant?'
he pushed.

'We—'

'Here you are,' Gibson said as he walked back into the
kitchen. He laid the plan on the table. 'This shows the
whole farm and I've highlighted the area comprising the
development. As you can see, there was a row of hedges
going from one side of the field to the other, and several
clumps of trees.' He pointed with his finger to the line on
the map.

'It appears the bodies were buried under the hedges.'
That made more sense.

'That's entirely possible,' he said.

What's that line mean?' she asked pointing to an area running to the left of the hedges.

'That's a public right of way. When drawing up the plans for the houses it had to be considered.'

Damn. That was a nuisance as it meant any number of people could have access to the burial site.

'Thank you for your help. We'll need to talk to you again, once we've been to see the pathologist and have more information about the bodies.'

'Do you have any idea when I can start the digging again?'

How many times did he have to ask? Did he think she was going to change her mind because he'd given her some help?

'We'll be in touch as soon as you can resume. I'm sorry, that's all I can say at the moment.'

They left the house and headed back towards Brian's car.

'Back to the station now, guv? I could do with cleaning my shoes and trousers.'

'Not yet. First, we're going to visit the morgue. We need their input before we can take this further.'

Chapter 4

'Are we seeing anyone in particular?' Brian asked as they were driving to the hospital.

'I called ahead and have arranged for us to see Claire.'

'Claire?'

'Dr Dexter. She's one of our pathologists. She's the best in the county, probably the country judging by the number of job offers and media interview requests she gets.'

'Ahead of those used by the Met?' He turned to her, his eyebrow arched.

'Yes, even ahead of them.'

Would Claire subject him to some of her *special* treatment? It was always fun to watch. It was a rite of passage for everyone who worked closely with the pathologist. She smiled to herself at the thought of their meeting.

After parking, they walked in through the double doors of the morgue and she wrinkled her nose as the smell hit her.

'I'm assuming you've been to the morgue plenty of times before,' she said to Brian.

'Not that many,' he admitted.

'Does that mean you haven't seen many dead bodies?'

'I've seen my fair share at dump sites, but visiting the morgue was usually left to my gaffers.'

'We work closely with Dr Dexter, so I imagine you'll be seeing her often.'

They walked into the lab and turned right into the office area. Claire was standing beside a man in a white coat, engrossed in conversation.

'Sorry to interrupt,' Whitney said.

'You're early,' Claire said in her usual officious manner.

'Only ten minutes. We can leave, get a coffee and come back when you're ready,' Whitney said, not at all upset at the thought of a caffeine fix.

'No need. This is Dr Leon de Villiers, he's the forensic anthropologist who's assisting in the analysis of the remains. I asked him to be here once I knew you were coming.'

'DCI Whitney Walker,' she said, holding out her hand to shake his. 'And this is my new sergeant, DS Chapman,' she said, turning back to Claire and gesturing to Brian.

'What happened to Matt?' Claire asked.

'He's moved to a smaller force so he could spend more time with his baby.'

Claire stared at Brian. 'I have rules.'

'You too?' Brian said, tossing a glance at Whitney.

She resisted the urge to rub her hands together in glee, as that would be way too childish. But this was definitely going to be fun.

'Yes. When you're in my lab, you do exactly as you're told.'

'Got it,' he said.

She turned to Whitney. 'We'll tell you what we have so far. Follow us.'

Whitney walked behind Claire and Dr de Villiers,

laughing to herself at the pathologist's glittery pink tights and red ankle boots. Beneath her white coat, she glimpsed a few inches of a green and white checked skirt.

On two of the stainless-steel tables in the centre of the lab were the remains laid out as they would be in a body. The bones had been cleaned and there was no mud on them. Whitney had never worked with just bones before, it didn't feel like a *normal* post-mortem.

'These are the reconstructed skeletons of the two bodies found at the farm,' Leon said.

'Can you tell what caused their deaths?' Brian asked.

'Wait until we invite questions,' Claire snapped.

Brian glanced at Whitney and she looked away, pretending she hadn't heard. How she managed not to laugh out loud was anyone's guess.

'Both skeletons are complete, and I've established they are female. If you look at the skull, you can see that the frontal bone is rounded.' He pointed to the skull of one of them. 'A male frontal bone is less rounded and slopes backwards at a gentler angle. The pelvic bones are another indicator if skulls are too damaged, which these aren't.'

Whitney peered at the body and nodded. 'What about their ages?'

'There are several methods of determining the age a person was at the time of their death. Our two bodies were teenagers, and I'd put them at around sixteen years old from measuring the length of the long bones in the leg. Teeth are another, more reliable, measure of estimating the age of a body, providing the person was under twenty-one. I checked the teeth on these two and it confirmed my original conclusion that both were sixteen.'

'How do you age skeletons on older bodies?' Whitney asked, her curiosity piqued.

'We can look at the fourth rib.' He pointed to the rib in

question on the body they were looking at. 'Over time, the cartilage between the end of the rib and the sternum turns to bone.' She moved in closer to see better.

'How long ago did these girls die?' Whitney asked.

'We took soil samples from around the bodies and there were several wool fibres found that most likely came from the clothes they were wearing. We're awaiting confirmation, but I'd place their deaths between the late 1970s and early 1980s.'

'Am I allowed to ask how they were killed yet?' Brian asked.

'Stop jumping the gun and making unsubstantiated claims,' Claire snapped. 'We don't as yet have confirmation that they were murdered. Cause of death could have been natural. They might have been walkers who got lost and curled up in freezing weather and weren't found.'

'Sorry,' Brian muttered.

'Leon, what can you tell us?' Whitney asked, keeping her voice neutral.

'What we have here are two healthy, teenage girls with no signs of disease, or illness, and no obvious cause of death. Also, there's nothing significant to identify them and although dental records could be used, without a name, and nothing of note on their teeth to ask dentists to look for in their records, we have a needle in a haystack situation. There are no broken bones that could be chased in hospital records. In summary, there's nothing obvious to identify them. We've sent bone fragments for testing and DNA extraction, but with bones this old, it could take a while to get a result. And if it turns out that their DNA isn't in the database then it will be up to you to identify them,' Leon said.

'If they'd been poisoned, would that show?' Whitney asked.

'Although we can identify certain diseases by deposits left in bones, unfortunately we can't tell if they'd been drugged or poisoned, unless there is any hair left on the body. Certain poisons leave markers in hair follicles, however, there are none on these ladies.'

'Thank you, we now have more to work on.' Whitney turned to Brian. 'I'll meet you in the car, I'd like a quick word with Dr Dexter.'

'About what?' Brian said, his eyes flashing.

'Nothing to do with the case. It's personal.'

'Okay,' he muttered, heading away from them.

'I'll leave you to it,' Leon said, walking back to the office and leaving the two of them alone.

'What is it?' Claire asked. 'I don't mix work and pleasure, you know that.'

'I wanted to know how married life was treating you.' Claire had married in secret a few months ago, and Whitney knew very little of her husband apart from that they'd met online. Not from a dating agency, as she'd first assumed when Claire told her. It turned out they were both on a committee arranging a research conference.

'It's fine, thank you.'

'Is that it? Just fine?'

She was beginning to regret the question, then again, she'd always been fairly similar to George in the *playing her cards close to her chest* stakes.

'It's very good, thank you.'

'What about Ralph and work?'

Claire's new husband was also a pathologist. He lived in Yorkshire and Whitney had been worried Claire would move up there, but she hadn't.

'He's been offered a position in Birmingham and he starts next week.'

'Thank goodness. Does that mean you're definitely going to stay here with us?' She smiled broadly.

'For now, yes. I have to get on, three bodies are due this morning. Goodbye.'

Whitney grinned, and she left the lab and headed down the corridor. As she passed the coffee machine, she stopped, gazing longingly. Should she get one? No. Brian was already agitated at being sent out. She wouldn't keep him waiting any longer.

When she reached his car, he was leaning against it tapping his foot on the ground.

'What are you doing out here in the cold?' she asked.

'Waiting for you.'

'You could have done that inside the car, instead of out here freezing your whatsits off.'

He shifted from one foot to the other. Was he building up to speak his mind? She suspected so.

'Look, I might be talking out of line, but I don't appreciate the way Dr Dexter spoke to me, nor the way you let her get away with it,' he blurted out.

She'd known he would have something to say about Claire but hadn't reckoned on getting the blame for allowing it to happen. She supposed he was right, but it wasn't like he was the only one to get the Claire treatment.

'It's not a question of *letting her get away with it*. It's Claire being Claire. She's the same with everyone, whether you're the chief constable, or—'

'A lowly sergeant,' he interrupted. 'But just so as you know, I don't intend to stay one for long. I'm on the way up.'

Whitney stifled a grin. She was beginning to get the measure of her new sergeant. 'What you've got to understand is we've worked with Claire for many years and we know her little idiosyncrasies. She enjoys intimidating people. Don't let it get to you. We're lucky to have her and she's a huge help in the solving of our cases.'

'So you said,' Brian muttered. 'No pathologist I've come across in the past has acted like her.'

'And I dare say they weren't as good as Claire either. So just cut her some slack and forget about it,' Whitney said.

'Okay, but for the record, I'm not happy about it.'

'Duly noted.'

'One more thing,' he said.

'What now?' She gave an exasperated sigh.

'What's with the clothes?'

Whitney laughed. That question she'd allow. 'Something else you'll get used to with Claire. She wears the most outlandish outfits and I seriously have no idea where she gets them from. But it's all part of her charm. Now, if you've finished, let's get back to the station as we need to track down the identities of the dead girls.'

Chapter 5

Whitney pushed open the door and headed to where her old whiteboard stood. She leant against the empty desk in front of it and called the team to attention. 'We've just come back from visiting the crime scene. It's an expanse of open fields, but the farmer did give me a plan showing what it was like before the digging started.' She stuck the plan to the board. 'This is where the bodies were found.' She pointed to the spot on the map.

'Guv,' Brian interrupted. 'You don't need to do that. I can scan the plan into the system, and we can put it up electronically for everyone to see.'

'No need. Once I've finished talking, you can scan it in if you wish.' She knew she had to learn to use the new electronic whiteboard, but at the moment she wanted to talk about the case without having to go through all the hassle of uploading the map. 'Anyway, the bodies were buried close to where originally there was a line of hedges, and next to a public right of way. That means any number of people would be able to access the farm and identify somewhere to bury the victims. We have been to see the pathologist, and—'

'Dr Dexter?' Frank interrupted.

'Yes.'

'Has she changed her name since she got married?'

'Not that I know of. Why?' She failed to see why it was relevant, but no doubt Frank would have a reason.

'I just wondered. What did you think of her, Sarge?' he asked Brian.

That was it. He wanted to know what had happened at the morgue. Frank was so transparent.

'I'm sure I'll get used to her,' he replied, casting a side-ways glance at Whitney.

'Frank, end the discussion on Dr Dexter and focus. According to the forensic anthropologist, Dr Leon de Villiers, who is working with Claire on the case, the bones belong to two sixteen-year-old girls.'

Silence hung over them. It always did when crimes against children were discovered.

'Crap,' Doug said, echoing everyone's thoughts.

'There were no visible signs of how they died, which he believes was around 1980. We're waiting to find out if there are any DNA matches in the database. Doug and Meena, you were looking at double missing persons cases, did you find anything?'

'Nothing useful, guv, as we didn't look as far back as that.'

'No problem. Ellie, I want you to look into all cases of missing teenage girls from the late 70s to early 80s. We may have to identify our bodies by a process of elimination.'

'Yes, guv,' Ellie said.

'I can help with that,' Brian said.

'Okay. The rest of you, anything come up regarding the farm?'

'The farm has been owned by the same family for over a hundred years, going back through the generations,' Doug said.

'Yes, Gibson mentioned they'd farmed there for a hundred and fifty years.'

'More recently, they've had to remortgage the farm itself.'

'Interesting. Gibson said they'd had some financial difficulties, and that's why they went down the route of using the land for housing. He hadn't mentioned them remortgaging farm, only that he applied for a mortgage for the development, which he referred to as being a *financial backstop*. This suggests it was more than that.'

'It seems unlikely that the family would be involved in burying the bodies,' Doug said.

'What makes you say that?' Whitney asked.

'If it was somebody at the farm who knew the bodies were there, they would have chosen different land to develop, or moved the bodies prior to all the excavation.'

'It's something to consider, but it's way too early to discount them. It could have been someone who's no longer around. Or someone who had worked for them back then. Frank, I want you to look into all family members, past and present. Right now, Anthony lives in the main farmhouse with his wife, their fifteen-year-old twin sons, and his father.'

'I've already established there are no police records relating to Gibson or his family,' Frank said.

'Keep digging, find out about who lived there before Anthony as he only took over twenty years ago. Meena, I want you to look into all employees going back at least fifty years. I'd like to have that information before we interview Gibson again.'

'Yes, guv.'

'As soon as you have any significant information, let me know,' she said to all of them. 'I'll be in my office if you need me.'

She returned to her desk and stared at her computer screen. It would take time to get used to the different atmosphere from having new people on the team. She'd only been seated for ten minutes when she saw Ellie heading in her direction.

'I've got something,' the officer said as she opened the door. 'Two sixteen-year-old girls from Lenchester were reported missing in May 1980.'

'And what happened to them?'

'That's the strange thing. Nothing. They were reported missing, and that's all there is on record. No update on whether they were found. It's very poor record-keeping.'

'You'll probably find all the information you need in the paper files. Only the basics would have been put into digital format. We're talking decades ago, remember. You'll need to locate the original files and see what else is in there.'

'I'll need a requisition form completing before the records department will release them to me.'

'I'll email it to them straight away. Knowing records, though, it will take a while before we get access to them. Assuming that they're all in the correct place following the move, and what's the betting they aren't?' she said grinning.

'I'm with you on that,' Ellie said, nodding.

'Without knowing anything more than they were reported missing, we should work on the assumption that the bodies could be them, so find out what you can about the disappearances. Were there any other teen girls reported missing at the same time?'

'There were some, but they were either on their own or

eventually found. This was the only report of two girls going missing together, not just around the same time, they were best friends and just disappeared one day.'

It was certainly pointing to them, but without DNA evidence it would just be supposition.

'Let me have their names and families' contact details. I'm assuming you've already got them.' She knew how Ellie worked.

'I'll text them to you. The girls are Jayne Kennedy, parents Nancy and Don. Anita Bailey, parents Gwen and Toby. Both families still live in the area.'

That was a bonus.

'Good work, Ellie.'

They returned to the incident room, and Whitney wrote their names on the board. 'Ellie's found records of two missing girls from 1980. The files are sparse to say the least and we're going to requisition the originals from archives. Brian, first thing in the morning you and I will visit the families. We need some DNA to test. We can test the parents or, if they have kept anything, something belonging to the girls themselves.'

Chapter 6

Whitney opened the email she'd just received from the pathology department and sighed. The missing girls weren't in the DNA database. She wasn't surprised as DNA wasn't collected so routinely all those years ago. She stood, intending to head into the incident room, and caught sight of Brian taking off his coat and hanging it on the coat stand. She glanced at her watch. It was after nine. Her eyes met with his and she beckoned him to her office.

'Morning, guv,' he said, closing the door behind him.

'I expected to see you earlier than this. Had you forgotten we're going to go visit the families?'

'No, I hadn't but we can't go too early. We have to give the parents time to get up and dressed.'

'We don't operate strict office times, as we often work late, however you were the last person to arrive this morning. It doesn't look good for a sergeant. I expect you to be in first in the future.'

'Sorry. I had something to deal with. It won't happen again.'

She wasn't going to pry into his private life. He'd

confide in her if he needed to and unless it affected his work, it wasn't her problem.

'Okay. We'll leave at ten. When you go into the incident room ask Meena to come in to see me.'

She'd speak to her first before going in to see the rest of the team, to allow Brian a chance to sort himself out.

'Is there anything wrong?' he asked, holding the door handle.

'No. Should there be?'

'I worked with Meena at Willsden and was surprised to see her assigned to this team.'

'Why?' Was there something she should know?

'She's conscientious and does whatever is asked of her, but that's about it. From my experience, you should know that she seldom shows initiative. I was *sold* this position based on it being a high-profile team with you at the helm. Senior management recognise you as a *case solver*. It's going to be my stepping-stone to promotion.'

He was *sold* the position. That was the first she'd heard of it. And why wasn't she given the choice whether to have him on the team? Whose ear did he have?

'We can't all be high-flyers within a team, or it wouldn't be very effective. I'm sure Meena will be fine with the right guidance … which I'm trusting you will give.'

'Yes, guv.'

'Thank you. I understand that coming into a team where two thirds of the members know each other isn't easy, but it will soon settle, for everyone.'

'Yes, guv. I'll send her in.'

She watched him go over to Meena. Whatever he said, she glanced at Whitney appearing panicked. Then she hurried over and knocked on Whitney's door, even though she could see Whitney was looking at her.

'Come in. Close the door behind you.'

The rest of the team were watching. It was going to take time to get used to the goldfish bowl she'd found herself in. There was the option to keep the blind closed, but that would separate her too much from the team. She'd work it out.

'Is there a problem, guv?' Meena asked, standing by the desk her fists balled by her side.

'Sit down. I wanted to ask how your first day went yesterday, that's all. It's just a friendly chat.'

The officer visibly breathed a sigh of relief and sat on the chair in front of Whitney's desk. 'It's all new, but it seemed okay. There's a good atmosphere and I like the other team members, but …' her voice tailed off.

'But?' Whitney pushed.

'I was just surprised to be on the same team as the sarge. He doesn't think I'm good at my job.'

'What makes you say that?'

'It was the impression I got at Willsden from odd remarks he'd made.'

'That's in the past. Remember, you're a part of *my* team, now and I judge people from what I observe myself, and not what others tell me. I'm sure you'll do well here. Frank, Doug and Ellie have worked together for a long time. They all have excellent abilities and bring something different to the team. Stick with them and you'll be just fine.'

'Thanks, guv,' Meena said, giving a smile of relief as she stood and returned to the incident room.

Whitney watched her make a beeline for Doug. She sat beside him, and they began talking.

At five minutes to ten, she went into the incident room. 'Pathology has emailed to let me know the girls aren't in the DNA database. It's up to us to identify them. Brian and I are visiting the families of the missing girls Ellie found yesterday. Hopefully, that will produce something.' She headed over to Brian's desk. 'Are you ready?'

'Yes, guv.'

They headed out of the station to his car. 'We'll go to the Kennedy house first, in Landcross Road.'

'You're clutching at straws if you think they're going to have anything belonging to their daughter after all this time,' Brian said.

Spoken like a person who didn't have children.

'Don't bank on it. When a parent loses a child, it's life altering. I've heard of people keeping their dead child's room in the exact state as it was when they'd died, for years after. Remember, if all else fails, we can take a DNA sample from the parents. One way or another, we will find out whether their children are our victims.'

'Yes, guv.'

'Do you have any children, Brian?' she asked, to clarify what she'd previously thought.

'No. I'm not even in a serious relationship. I've got more important things to concentrate on.'

She understood the desire to be career focused. Since joining the force at eighteen, after having her daughter Tiffany, she'd put all of her energy into her career. Although ... recently she'd rekindled her friendship with Tiffany's father, who she hadn't spoken to since she'd left school. Her daughter had no idea Whitney had met him, as she'd been in Australia for almost a year.

Whitney hoped to see Tiffany at Christmas. Then she'd drop the bombshell. She had no idea how Tiffany would take it. Whitney had only ever referred to the conception happening one drunken night, with a *waste of space loser*. It turned out that Martin was anything but. Deep down, Whitney was hoping their relationship might develop into something more serious. If she had time. Which reminded her, she was going to call him later to invite him down for the weekend.

'I get where you're coming from. But remember, there's more to life than the job,' she said.

'Not at my age.'

'Well, just make sure life doesn't pass you by. The years go so quickly. One day you're in your twenties, and the next you're knocking on forty, without the faintest idea where the time went.'

'I take it you're speaking from experience,' he said, a wry grin on his face.

'Something like that. We want twenty-six Landcross Road.'

He keyed the address into the satnav and they drove to the small Victorian terraced house in the St James area of the city.

They parked on the road outside and walked up the short path to the door. Whitney shivered and pulled her coat tightly around her. She hated the cold and couldn't wait for winter to be over. Two minutes after she'd rung the bell, an elderly woman in her seventies answered.

'Mrs Kennedy?' Whitney asked.

'Yes.'

'I'm Detective Chief Inspector Walker and this is Detective Sergeant Chapman.' She held out her warrant card. 'We'd like to come in and talk to you about your daughter, Jayne.'

The woman's eyes widened. 'What?'

'Your daughter, Jayne.'

'Yes, I know who you mean, but why do you want to talk now? She disappeared years ago.'

'We'd rather discuss this inside. Is Mr Kennedy here?'

'Yes, he's in the lounge. Come on in.' Mrs Kennedy opened the door and ushered them inside.

'Thank you.'

They followed her into the lounge where Mr Kennedy was seated at one end of the black leather sofa reading the newspaper.

'It's the police, Don,' Mrs Kennedy said. 'They're here about Jayne.'

He dropped his newspaper and jumped up. 'Why?'

'Please will you sit down.' She waited until they were both seated on the sofa before sitting on the leather chair to the side of them. She nodded for Brian to wait by the window as there wasn't another chair.

'I know it's been many years, but we are investigating the discovery of two bodies at a farm in the area—'

Mrs Kennedy gasped and clutched at her chest. 'Do you think it's Jayne?'

'It's early stages, and we don't yet have a formal identification. All we know is the victims were both girls aged around sixteen. Records show that you reported Jayne missing at the time we believe the girls died.'

She didn't want to use the word *murdered* yet as they didn't know how they'd died, even though it was most likely that's what had happened.

'T-the police wouldn't listen to us. They were convinced the girls had run away, and we kept insisting they hadn't, but no one believed us. Did they?' She looked at her husband who was staring directly at Whitney, his face set like stone.

'Did you have any contact with Jayne and her friend Anita after they'd disappeared?'

'No. The police were adamant they'd run away to London. They said they'd been seen at the station waiting for a train.'

Whitney would investigate that. Unfortunately, they

didn't have the luxury of CCTV on every street corner all those years ago.

'Is there anything else you can tell us about what happened? We haven't yet got the files out of storage so your input could help speed up the investigation and identification of the remains.'

'After the police refused to listen to us, we decided to look for the girls ourselves. We couldn't sit back and wait like they told us to. We put notices in the newspapers and stuck up leaflets in the library and on lamp posts. B-but no one came forward. It was like they'd never existed, they …' The woman choked on her words.

'Did the police help with the search?' Whitney asked gently.

'No. In fact, they told us to stop wasting our time. They said they'd come home when they were ready,' Mr Kennedy said, taking over as his wife silently sobbed.

'Did Anita's parents help you?' Whitney asked.

'Half-heartedly,' Mr Kennedy said. 'They believed the police.'

The pain in his voice was almost tangible. It wrenched at Whitney's gut.

'Did Jayne have any money on her on the day she disappeared?' Whitney asked.

'I think she did,' Mrs Kennedy said, after sniffing. 'All she took with her that day was her handbag. After she'd gone and I was searching her bedroom for something to help us find her, I found her building society book and saw that a few days prior she'd taken most of the money out of it.'

'How much did she have?'

'Two hundred pounds. She'd been saving since she was a child.'

'That was a lot of money all those years ago. Did you mention it to the police?' Whitney asked.

'No, because we thought it would stop them looking for her. But they stopped anyway.' She bowed her head. 'We kept telling them she wouldn't have run away. Also, why didn't she take any clothes with her? Surely if she'd planned to leave home, she'd have taken more than her handbag.'

What on earth were the investigating officers doing? Mrs Kennedy was right, they would definitely have taken some clothes with them.

'For us to identify whether one of the bodies we've found is Jayne, we ideally need something with her DNA on it. Did you, by any chance, keep anything of hers?'

Mrs Kennedy glanced at her husband. 'In the loft we have a box of Jayne's possessions,' he said.

'Could you get it for us, please?' Whitney asked.

'I'll help,' Brian said.

He left the room with Mr Kennedy.

'Do you have any other children?' Whitney asked.

'Yes, a daughter, Natasha, she was three years younger than Jayne.'

'Does she live close by?' After the shock the elderly couple had just received, Whitney would have liked them to have someone with them.

'She lives in Norwich with her family.'

'Would you like us to contact her for you?'

'No, thank you. You don't know for sure if this is Jayne and I don't want to worry her until we know for certain. If it is, can we have a funeral for her? It would help.'

'You can, but we have to wait until the coroner has completed her investigation and given permission for your daughter to be returned to you. Will you tell me about the girls?'

'Jayne wasn't perfect and was often in trouble. But she was also loving and kind. The two girls were best friends and inseparable. Anita was the bossy one, and she often persuaded Jayne to do things I'm sure she wouldn't have done otherwise.'

Whitney went on alert. Had they been involved in something which caused them to lose their lives?

'When you say she was often in trouble, what sort of things did they get up to?'

'They were caught stealing sweets from the local newsagents,' Mrs Kennedy said.

Hardly worth getting killed over.

'Were they punished?'

'No. Luckily, they just got a warning, and the police weren't involved.'

'How did you find out?'

'We knew the newsagent, and he contacted us. We promised him it wouldn't happen again. Jayne was very upset by the whole thing and we thought she'd learnt her lesson.'

'What about at school? Did she work hard? Did she behave?'

'She was a typical sixteen-year-old. More interested in boys and going out with her friends.'

The door opened and Mr Kennedy walked in followed by Brian carrying a large brown box, which he placed on the floor in front of Mrs Kennedy.

'I haven't looked in here for years. We didn't keep everything of Jayne's, just a few things to remind us of her.' She hesitated before opening the box and drew in a deep breath. 'What do you need to do your test?'

'A hairbrush or comb, which would have some of her hairs on it,' Whitney said, her heart going out to the woman having to go through her daughter's possessions after so many years, especially in front of strangers.

Mrs Kennedy rummaged through the box and pulled out a hair tie. She scrutinised it. 'No brush, but this has her hairs on it. Will that help?'

'Yes, thank you.' Whitney took it from her and dropped it into an evidence bag. 'What else is in the box? Did Jayne keep a diary?'

'Yes, there are diaries and notebooks and some of her favourite furry animals.'

'Please may we take the box with us?' Whitney asked gently. 'We'll look after everything and return it once we've finished.'

Mrs Kennedy looked at her husband. He nodded. 'Yes,' he said.

'Thank you. Do you have a photo of Jayne we can take with us?'

Mr Kennedy went over to the oak sideboard running along the back wall. He opened the middle drawer and pulled out a photo.

'This is one of Jayne taken a couple of months before she disappeared. It was at her sister's birthday party.' He held the photo out and Whitney took it from him.

She was a pretty girl, with a happy face and dimples in her cheeks. Whitney's body tensed. What the hell happened?

'I'll let you have this back as soon our investigation is completed.'

'Is there anything else we can help you with?' Mr Kennedy asked.

'Are you sure there was nothing going on at home which would have caused your daughter to run away?' Brian asked.

Whitney sucked in a breath. The right question, but definitely not the right time to ask it.

'What do you mean?' Mr Kennedy asked.

'Fights, arguments. Anything that made her not want to come home.'

'She fought with her sister sometimes, but nothing out of the ordinary and no different from any other sisters.'

'What about with you and Mrs Kennedy? Had *you* fought with her before she went?'

'No.'

'Are you absolutely sure about that?' Brian pushed.

'Yes,' he said, voice tight as his mouth formed a flat line. 'It all happened out of the blue. We had no warning, that's why we know she didn't run away.'

'We'll be going now,' Whitney said, not wanting the questioning to continue.

They left the house and returned to the car.

'Next one?' Brian asked.

Didn't he have anything to say about the interview? Wasn't he affected by it at all? He was an unmarried child-less male; was that the reason? Whitney dragged in a breath and nodded.

'Yes. The Baileys live at 349 Wellington Street, Far Cotton. It's twenty minutes away. They've moved since the girls disappeared.'

'Okay, guv.'

Whitney waited until they were on the road and in traffic before she turned to Brian.

'You don't seem to have grasped my instructions. Interviews are led by me.' She kept her voice calm but cold.

'What if I come up with a question that you haven't asked?' he said.

'I might not have deemed it the right moment to ask. I like to run interviews in a certain way.'

'We were about to leave, and you hadn't questioned them about their relationship with their daughter. Surely you must have considered that to be important.'

'I'd been talking to Mrs Kennedy when you were out of the room and we had discussed Jayne's behaviour. Your attitude put them on the back foot. It was as if you were accusing them of having something to do with the deaths.'

A slight exaggeration, but he needed to understand that they did things her way.

'They could have done. Murders are often committed by people known to the victims.'

He was correct, but other factors had to be considered before leaping to conclusions.

'I agree, but when investigating it's often advisable not to alert potential suspects. They're elderly people who looked for their daughter for months, pursuing every avenue they could. Is that the behaviour of murderers?'

'They could have done it to put the police off the scent,' Brian said.

'The police had already gone *off the scent.* Just leave it to me during the next interview. I'll do the talking and you listen.' She drew in a frustrated breath. She'd cut him some slack once, as he wasn't used to working in this way. But now he knew she didn't intend to be so accommodating.

'Yes, guv. I'll try to remember.'

Try. He'd better do more than that.

Chapter 7

They remained silent for the rest of the journey, and soon Brian pulled up outside a 1930s semi-detached pebble-dashed house.

An older woman, wearing a stained floral apron, opened the door. Her grey hair was pulled off her face and streaks of flour were smeared across her forehead.

'Mrs Bailey?' Whitney asked.

'Yes.'

'I'm Detective Chief Inspector Walker and this is Detective Sergeant Chapman. We'd like to speak to you about your daughter, Anita.'

Colour leached from her face. 'Have you found her?'

'Please, may we come in?' Whitney said, her voice gentle. 'We don't really want to talk out here.'

The woman stepped to the side allowing them space to enter. 'Of course. I'm in the kitchen baking. It's my grandson's tenth birthday in a couple of days and I'm making him a train cake. He's obsessed by them.' The words tumbled out of her mouth.

Nerves?

'Is Mr Bailey here?'

'We divorced a long time ago. I haven't seen him since he moved to the States in 2005. Come on through to the kitchen I need to keep an eye on my timer.'

They followed her into the small kitchen, and sat at the round wooden dining table.

'Mrs Bailey.'

'Please, call me Gwen,' she said.

'We've come to see you because two bodies have been found on a building site close to town. The forensic pathologist has informed us they are two sixteen-year-old girls and we're investigating whether they could be Anita and Jayne.'

The woman grabbed hold of the table. Her knuckles white. 'Are you sure? We thought they'd run away, that's what the police told us.'

'Did you believe that's what had happened?'

'I wasn't sure, but it seemed likely.'

'Jayne's parents didn't think so.'

'I know, but they didn't know the half of what the girls got up to. Even before they disappeared, I had the feeling they were planning something.'

'Could you explain?'

'They were out of control, especially Anita. She was in trouble at school and ignored everything we said. It was a hard time for us. If she spoke to us, which was rarely, she was usually rude.'

'Mr and Mrs Kennedy mentioned about some shoplifting at a local newsagent, and that Jayne had promised not to do it again.'

'They were way worse than that. They used to go into town every Saturday, and I'm fairly sure they stole from shops. I'm surprised they didn't get caught.'

'How did you know what they were doing?'

'I found a stash of expensive, unworn, clothes in Anita's room, which no way could she have afforded as she didn't have a job. The only thing I could think of was shoplifting. At least, that's what I told myself. I couldn't bear for it to be anything else.'

'Did you question her about it?'

She shook her head. 'I didn't want to risk another blow up, so I turned a blind eye. I know it was wrong, but by that time I was at the end of my tether. Everything the girls did was instigated by Anita. She was the stronger of the two and Jayne went along with it. She was a nice girl, always polite when she was here, despite witnessing the way Anita treated us.'

'I know it's a long time ago, but could you run through what happened on the day the girls went missing,' Whitney said.

'Nancy Kennedy phoned wanting to know if Jayne was with us because she'd been expecting her home for tea. I'd just assumed Anita was with them and when we discovered they were missing we went to the police together. They interviewed us but came to the conclusion they'd run away because someone had seen them near the station.'

'The Kennedys put out leaflets and searched for the girls. Did you do the same?'

'I did help them but, to be honest, after the police told us they were spotted at the station, I thought they'd run away. But now you're telling me they might not have. I just...' Her voice faded.

'At the moment, we're trying to identify the bodies. Do you have anything of Anita's, like an old hairbrush, we could use to take her DNA and compare it to the bodies we have discovered?'

'I didn't keep anything of Anita's after moving here

twenty years ago, when I split with Toby. All I have now are photos.'

How different the two families were.

'Would you mind giving us a sample of your DNA? We can check that way,' Whitney asked.

'Of course. I can't believe they didn't run away ... that they could have been dead all this time.' She leant forward and rested her chin in her hand. 'If only I'd known.'

'We don't know for definite, it's early in the investigation.' Whitney took a DNA testing kit out of her bag and removed the cotton swab. 'Please could you open your mouth?' She applied the tip of the swab to the inside of the woman's mouth and rubbed lightly while turning the swab to make sure the whole of the tip had made contact with the area.

'How long will it take for the results to come back?' Gwen asked.

'We'll try to rush it through. How many other children do you have?'

'Two, a son and a daughter. One is older than Anita and the other is younger.'

'How were they during the time when Anita went missing?'

Gwen coloured. 'Life was much easier when she wasn't here. My son, the oldest, was always exceptionally good at school and we had no trouble with him. He's now a doctor. My younger daughter is easy-going and Anita bullied her. She blossomed once Anita left. I really believed she'd run away. I hate myself for saying this, but when it happened ... it was a relief.'

'She was only sixteen and you're acting like you were pleased she'd run away. You do know how runaways support themselves in places like London, don't you?' Brian jumped in.

'I-I …' Gwen's eyes pleaded with Whitney for support.

'Mrs Bailey, Gwen. We're not accusing you of anything,' Whitney said gently.

'She had money. I thought she'd be okay.'

'How much?' Whitney asked.

'A few hundred pounds. I found the money in her bedroom a few weeks before she went missing, and it wasn't there after she'd gone. I loved my daughter, you have to believe me but …' Tears fell down her cheeks and Whitney picked up a box of tissues from the side and passed it to her.

'Were you concerned when you didn't hear from Anita at all?' Whitney asked.

'Initially, I expected her to call. It gradually got easier, the longer it went without her contacting us. You must think me an awful person.'

'Not at all. We all react differently to situations,' Whitney said, hoping she was reassuring the woman, because in truth she couldn't comprehend such a reaction.

'If it does turn out to be Anita, I'll have to get in touch with her father so we can have a funeral. I'm assuming we can have one.'

'Yes, once the coroner releases Anita's body, after the autopsy has been completed. The coroner's office will be in contact with you at that time.'

It was strange calling the skeletal remains a body, but she could hardly say bones.

'Can you tell us a bit more about how Anita was out of control,' Brian said.

Whitney froze. The woman had just been given the news her daughter had possibly been dead for decades. There was nothing else they needed at this stage. Their priority was to identify the bodies. There a niggling doubt at the back of her mind that Anita's parents could have been involved, if the situation was really that bad at home. But that wouldn't account for Jayne.

'I'm sure I don't know all that she got up to, apart from shoplifting and playing truant from school.'

'Did she fight with anyone? Did she get in trouble? Did she take drugs?' Brian pushed.

'I don't know. She was out of hand and we couldn't control her. She'd go out at night and not tell us where she was going. I don't know about drugs, it was too long ago.' She sniffed.

'Is there anyone we can contact to be with you?' Whitney asked.

'I'm fine on my own. I've got to finish this birthday cake. You've brought up so many memories. You never stop loving your children, whatever the circumstances.'

'But you didn't try to find her,' Brian said.

The woman bowed her head.

'Thank you for your time,' Whitney said. 'We'll be in touch to let you know the results of the test.'

They left the house and Whitney turned to Brian. 'I will not tell you again. That poor woman didn't need grilling, we're only at the stage of identifying the bodies.'

'If you say so, guv.'

'Yes. I do. In future, you will do as I say, or you won't be happy with the outcome.'

Chapter 8

'Would you like to go skiing over Christmas?' Dr Georgina Cavendish asked her partner Ross, as she sat opposite him at a table in the university café. He'd joined her for lunch as he'd been in the area visiting someone who'd commissioned a sculpture of their dog.

'Skiing? I'm not sure. I've only ever been once on a school trip and I spent more time on my arse than standing upright on skis.'

'We can ski on separate slopes and you can have some lessons while we're there. It would be pleasant to get away over the holidays.'

'This is the first time *you've* suggested going away together. Normally it's me wanting to make plans.'

They had only recently begun seeing each other again after six months apart, when he'd proposed and she'd turned him down. She'd ended the relationship and realised, almost immediately, that she'd made a mistake, but hadn't done anything about it. It wasn't until she'd seen him at an exhibition he'd held at a local gallery that they'd started seeing each other again.

He hadn't broached the topic of marriage or living together again, but if he did, she was beginning to warm to the idea. She might even mention it herself, rather than wait for him.

'Does it matter who suggests it?' She frowned.

'Not at all, I'd love to go away.'

'Let's go to Val d'Isère and rent a chalet. It will be perfect skiing weather.'

Skiing was her favourite pastime, but she rarely had the opportunity to go. She was either busy at the university with her lecturing and research, or helping Whitney and her team solve murder cases. When she was on the slopes, she could switch off and not think of anything other than reaching the bottom of the hill.

'Shall we go there over Christmas itself?'

'I've got the family Christmas lunch, remember. I have to see my parents, or they'll make a huge issue out of it.'

'Surely they won't mind if you miss it once.'

'It would be nice to not have to sit through it, I must admit.'

'We could visit both families pre-Christmas and hand out the presents. My parents would love to see you again.'

She'd enjoyed spending time with Ross's family in the past. They were easy to be with and didn't pressure her to make small talk. She could sit back and observe them all together.

'I'm not sure it's appropriate this year. If my father is given a prison sentence after his court case next year, there might not be another of our traditional lunches for a long time.'

Her father, along with many other high-profile people, had been charged with tax evasion. His court date was expected to be sometime next year.

'I understand. I can come with you, if you like?'

'No, I won't put you through the torture. Let's go skiing the day after Boxing Day and spend New Year over there.'

'Will we find anywhere to book with less than two weeks' notice?'

'It is a long shot, but I know someone with a chalet. I'll contact them to see if they're using it this year and, if they're not, I'm sure we'll be able to. I've been there before, and it's perfectly situated.'

'Sounds great.'

Her phone rang, and she glanced down at the screen. 'It's Whitney, I'd better answer this.' She accepted the call. 'Hello.'

'Hi, George, how are you? We haven't spoken in ages,' her friend said.

'I'm with Ross having lunch.' She glanced across at him. He was leaning back in his chair, smiling in her direction.

'You're not at work today?'

'Yes, I am. Ross met me here as he was in the city. The students have finished, and I've come in to complete my admin and prepare some research for publication next year. Did you want anything in particular? I can phone you later once I'm back in my office.'

If Whitney wanted to chat, they'd be on the phone for a while and it was rude to ignore Ross as he wouldn't be staying much longer.

'We have a new case I thought you'd be interested in.'

'Tell me more,' George said, sitting forward slightly, her curiosity piqued.

'The remains of two sixteen-year-old girls have been found on a farm. They've been there since 1980. We're in the process of identifying them and investigating their deaths.'

'What sort of help are you expecting from me?'

She knew a little forensic anthropology, but not enough to be of much assistance.

'We can always do with your input. I just thought you might enjoy coming in for a catch-up and to meet the new team.'

Ah … was that the *real* reason Whitney had called. Was she already having trouble with them?

'How is it working out?'

'Not bad. I'll tell you when I see you.'

'I'll be with you after we've finished lunch.'

'Great. Don't forget, we've moved into the new building. We're on the fifth floor. You'll have to report to the reception first and I'll come and get you. No more slipping in through the back door.'

'Extra security is a good thing,' George said.

'Agreed. Enjoy the rest of your lunch and I'll see you soon.'

George placed her phone back on the table and looked over at Ross. 'Whitney has a case she'd like my input on.'

'I gathered as much. We better hurry up and finish eating.'

'I don't want to rush you.'

'It's no trouble.'

She appreciated how understanding he was of her work with the police and how he'd never once made her feel guilty for missing dates or rushing off to a crime scene. He realised that criminals didn't wait for the investigators to have finished their dinner before committing crimes.

They ended their meal and after saying goodbye, George drove to the new station and parked in the visitors' car park as she didn't have a swipe card for the staff section. She walked into the new modern and clean building. Whitney had predicted that the building would lack character, because it had none of the charm of the Victorian building where they used to be based, and she was correct.

She made her way to the reception desk. 'Dr Georgina Cavendish to see DCI Walker.'

'Just one moment and I'll let her know you're here,' the woman on reception said.

George stepped to the side and observed the hive of activity around her. There were people heading in all directions. After a couple of minutes, one of the lift doors opened, and Whitney marched out. George hurried over to meet her.

'I need to get you a visitor's pass,' Whitney said as she hurried to the reception desk. 'I'd like a pass for Dr Cavendish.'

George frowned. 'Why am I classed as a visitor if I'm part of the team?'

'New procedures. I'll see about getting you a formal identification tag so you can come in and out without having to report here all the time, especially as you're going to continue working with us.'

The receptionist handed her a lanyard complete with pass, which George hung around her neck.

'Was there some doubt as to my position here?' she asked, as they headed towards the lift.

'I had to get permission from the new super for us to continue using you. What do you think to the station?'

'Utilitarian. It appears fit for purpose. Other than that, nothing about it stands out.'

'I agree. I've got more character in my little finger than this building has. But, as you said, it's functional and does its job.'

They took the lift to the fifth floor and walked along the corridor until reaching an office door with Whitney's name sign-written on it in gold letters.

'You no longer have to go through the incident room to get to your office, that gives you more privacy.'

'You'd like to think so, but no. There are two entrances, this one and one which goes into the incident room. Anyone in there gets a bird's-eye view of everything I'm doing.' Whitney opened the door, and they stepped inside.

'This is much larger than your previous office.'

'Larger, yes, but more like a goldfish bowl because it's so close to the team.'

George stared through the windows and could see some familiar faces sitting at their desks.

'I see what you mean,' she said.

'We'll sit at the coffee table, the only area where we can't be seen as it's off to the side,' Whitney said.

'Good idea,' she replied, pulling out a chair and sitting.

'How are you and Ross doing?' Whitney asked.

'Everything's going well. When you phoned, we were planning a skiing trip after Christmas.'

'That sounds fun. At least, I'm sure it will be for you. I've never been skiing nor wanted to.'

'What are you doing over Christmas?'

'I'm hoping Tiffany will make it home. She has hinted that she might, but you know what she's like. She's having such a good time. I can sense there's something going on but I can't put my finger on it.'

Was Tiffany in trouble? George had a soft spot for the young woman and would hate for there to be anything amiss.

'What do you mean?'

'Call it mother's instinct. She's happy and I think she might have met someone, but I don't like to ask.'

'Why ever not?' George said.

'She'll tell me when she's ready. But to be honest, I don't want to hear that she's met the love of her life and wants to stay out there. I'm closing my mind to it. Let's change the subject.'

'Tell me about the new members of your team,' George said. 'Are they managing to fit in?'

'It's early days but it's not easy. The other team … we were together for so long … we all knew each other well. But now the dynamics have changed.'

'You've still got Frank, Ellie and Doug, so surely it can't be too bad.'

'Yes, I have, thank goodness. My new sergeant, Brian, is going to take a bit of getting used to. He worked at the Met before moving to Willsden and views being part of the team as a stepping-stone onto greater things. I suspect that he won't be here for long. He's got it into his head he's on some sort of super squad. Where he got that idea from is anybody's guess.'

'What about the other new member?'

'Meena. She's very quiet, so I've yet to discover what she's like. She worked with Chapman before.'

'Are they sticking together?'

'No. He's already told me he doesn't rate her. I hope it doesn't lead to trouble, although I dare say one of the others will let me know if any issues arise between them.'

'Tell me about the case,' George said.

'We suspect the bodies found might be two girls who disappeared in 1980. The officers who investigated their disappearance seemed quick to label them as runaways, despite the parents of one girl insisting otherwise. We're waiting for the original investigation files to be sent through from the evidence store, although I suspect they might not contain much, as record-keeping was very different in those days.'

'At sixteen they were legally entitled to leave home, is

that why they assumed they'd run away, do you think?' George asked.

'I don't know. Sixteen might be the legal age for leaving home, but it's still young. It doesn't help that it took place in 1980 and there's no CCTV footage to help us.'

'What *do* you have to work with?' she asked.

'Nothing until the files arrive and we get a positive identification from the DNA samples we've sent for testing.'

'How did the parents take it?'

'Their reactions were interesting. Jayne's parents had kept many of her possessions. They were shocked, naturally, to learn what might have happened. Anita's mother was different, almost as though she didn't care, apart from one comment she made about never stopping loving your children, whatever they've done. We discovered that both girls were going off the rails, and they regularly shoplifted. Anita was the leader and, in particular, was out of control.'

'You have somewhere to start by the sounds of it. How long before the previous investigation files arrive?' George asked.

'I'm hoping today, tomorrow at the latest. I'll take you through to meet the new members of the team. The others will be pleased to see you. How long can you stay for?'

'As long as you need me.'

Chapter 9

Whitney opened the door into the incident room and led George in.

What would the new members of the team make of George?

When the forensic psychologist had first joined them a couple of years ago, the team had been wary. If it wasn't for Matt suggesting that they worked together, because he realised her expertise would help, then it might not have happened. Whitney, in particular, had issues with George initially and sparks had flown between them. They'd got over that a long time ago, but George could still be intimidating. She had a particular no-nonsense air about her and coupled with her five feet ten-inch height, which Whitney was jealous of, she was a force to be reckoned with.

The team had accepted her and now joked and chatted when she was around, although it could be a challenge as George didn't always understand humour and wasn't one for small talk.

But she couldn't imagine the team without her being a part of it.

They headed to the board and Whitney called the team to attention, waiting for them all to look in her direction. 'Brian and Meena, I would like to introduce you to Dr Cavendish. She's a forensic psychologist who works at the university and she's helped us solve many cases.'

'Hello,' Meena said, smiling.

'Why do we need a forensic psychologist to help us when we don't know who the victims or suspects are yet?' Brian asked.

'Because there's no one else like Dr Cavendish,' Frank piped up. 'There's nothing she doesn't know.'

'I wouldn't go that far, Frank,' George said.

'No need for modesty here, Dr C. Trust me, Sarge. We were always a *good* team, but with the doc on board we're a *super* team. You ask her a question. Anything. She'll have an answer.'

Whitney grinned. 'I think Frank has said it all.'

'When I was at the Met,' Brian said. Frank groaned and Whitney glared at him. 'We sometimes used forensic psychologists and had quite a few to call on but, quite frankly, we were usually more expert at solving crimes. We didn't need them.'

'That's not the case here. George has as much to offer as anyone else on the team, as I'm sure you'll find out. Let's have a catch-up on where we are,' Whitney said, deciding there had been enough discussion of George's use in the team. 'Ellie, the files?'

'As you thought, because of the move they haven't been easy to locate, but I've been promised they'll be with us by tomorrow morning.'

'Good. I want you to keep on top of it as we need to get cracking, not least because the new super will want an update and she may restrict the time we have to work on the case as it's from so long ago. Who went through the box belonging to Jayne Kennedy?'

'Me, guv,' Meena said. 'There are several diaries and, judging by the inscriptions, they'd been given to her each year by her parents. But there was nothing much recorded in them, just the occasional note regarding homework. The rest of the box contained some jewellery, old toys, colouring pictures from when she was a child, that kind of thing.'

'Is there anything else of importance on the farmer, Doug?'

'Nothing apart from the financial difficulties we already knew about. They're both model citizens. Anthony Gibson is an active member of the local Rotary club, and his wife is in the Women's Institute. There are no police records on anyone in the family, but I'll keep on digging, in case anything crops up,' Doug said.

'While we're waiting for DNA results, Meena, I want you to look into the Kennedy family, and Frank, you take the Bailey family. Mr Bailey is now living in the States, according to his ex-wife.'

'Yes, guv,' Frank and Meena said at the same time.

She glanced at George and nodded for her to come with her. They entered her office, closing the door behind them.

'What's your verdict on Brian and Meena?' she asked before they'd even sat down. She was interested in George's view.

'Meena is eager to be a fully contributing member of the team.'

'Agreed. What about Brian? I can't make up my mind about him.'

'In my opinion, he needs to settle in and find his feet.'

'You think he's trying to prove himself? Is that why he's questioning what I do?'

'That's part of it, but it also appears that you have more issues with men than women.'

What? Where did that come from?

'Meaning?' she said flatly.

'Look at your history. First you had Douglas, then Jamieson, and now Chapman.'

'I dispute that. What about my first boss, Don Mason, and also Matt, Doug, and Frank?'

'Don Mason aside, they are part of your team and are compliant, not confrontational, unlike the other males I mentioned. I'll be interested to see your behaviour with a superior female officer before I can make a final assessment.'

From anyone else, Whitney would have taken the comments as a slur against her character and been angry, but it was different as far as George was concerned. She said what she saw, without any desire to undermine or cause friction.

'I don't judge people on their gender. It just so happens there have been some males I've had issues with, and it was to do with them as people, nothing else.' It made perfect sense to her.

'When you spoke to Brian, your body language changed. You were tense, and the lines around your eyes tightened. It's exactly how you were when conversing with Jamieson.'

'Oh, stop being such a know-it-all,' Whitney said scowling, knowing inside that George was probably right.

'It's your responsibility to ensure that once he's settled, you have a good working relationship, or you will struggle.'

Whitney sighed. 'I know what you're saying, but I want him to come around to my way of working. Matt was so different, his interpersonal skills were excellent, and everyone liked him. He didn't question my judgement often, but if he did, it would make me re-evaluate the situation. We had a great working relationship.'

She hoped that Matt enjoyed his new force. He was the sort of officer to slot in and be accepted anywhere, so he no doubt would. She must remember to keep in touch as she'd love to know how the baby was getting on, though knowing how private Matt and Leigh were, she doubted she'd learn much.

'Now you've accepted my observations, I'm sure it will all be fine,' George said.

'I don't know Brian yet, but it will work out. I'll make sure it does,' she said with conviction. Hoping it wasn't misplaced.

'Good. What else are we to do today?' George asked.

'I'm not actually sure why I asked you to come in this afternoon, other than to meet the team and have a chat because we haven't seen each other in ages. We need to go back to the farm, but I don't want to do that until the victims have been identified.'

'Phone me when you want to go. I'm at work all week and can get away anytime you need me.'

'Great. I'll show you around the station before you go, and we can grab a coffee. You'll be impressed with our new cafeteria because, believe it or not, the coffee's not too bad. Maybe not to your standard, though, come to think of it,' Whitney added, knowing that she probably wasn't the best person to comment as she'd drink anything as long as it contained caffeine.

'I'll be the judge of that,' George said. .

Whitney grinned, grateful that at least some things hadn't changed. She might be in a new building with a new team, but George was still a coffee snob.

Chapter 10

Whitney opened the email from forensics which had just arrived in her inbox. It had been two days since the DNA samples had been sent over for comparison, and they'd rushed through the analysis as a favour to her. They now had confirmation that the bodies were indeed Jayne Kennedy and Anita Bailey. As awful as it was to correctly identify them, at least now they could get on with their work and discover how they died. First of all, though, she needed to let the parents know. It wasn't something she relished doing, but she hoped it would give them some long-awaited closure.

She sucked in a breath, picked up her phone and keyed in the first number. It was answered on the first ring.

'Is that Mr Kennedy?'

'Yes.'

'It's Detective Chief Inspector Walker.'

'Do you … have you some news for us?' he hesitated.

'Yes, I have. I'm sorry to have to inform you, but we have identified Jayne as one of the bodies buried on the farm.'

Silence hung in the air.

'Was the other one Anita?' he finally asked, his voice choked.

'I can't disclose who the other person was until we have spoken to their family.'

She was sure he'd realise it was Anita, it couldn't be anyone else.

'I understand,' he said.

'Is Mrs Kennedy at home?'

'Yes, she is. I'll tell her shortly. How did Jayne die? Was she murdered?'

That was what Whitney assumed, however, she wasn't going to tell Mr Kennedy that until they had more concrete evidence.

'The pathologist is still investigating. At the moment we don't know.'

'Can you tell me what's going to happen next?'

'The coroner will release Jayne to you once the investigations are over and then you'll be free to arrange her funeral.'

'Thank you for letting me know. I know it's been years, but I'd always hoped Jayne was still alive, even though she hadn't been in touch. That she might have had amnesia or something, but …'

Tears welled in Whitney's eyes, but she blinked them away. This wasn't her pain to deal with.

'I'm very sorry for your loss. If you do need to speak to me, phone any time, you've got my number. I'll do my best to keep you up to date with the investigation.'

'Thank you very much. We appreciate all you're doing.'

Whitney ended the call and drew in some calming

breaths before picking up the phone again. This time to contact Gwen Bailey, Anita's mother.

The woman answered almost immediately.

'It's Detective Chief Inspector Walker here.'

'Hello. Do you have news for me?'

Whitney relaxed her shoulders as she needed to come across as calm.

'Yes. I'm phoning to let you know that we've analysed the DNA sample you provided, and formally identified Anita as being one of the bodies we found at Oak Tree Farm. As yet, we don't know the cause of her death. I'm very sorry for your loss.'

'Thank you for letting me know,' the woman said, her voice matter-of-fact and clinical. 'You said that we could have the funeral after the autopsy, is that still the case?'

'Yes, it is. Someone from the coroner's office will contact you and let you know when that will be.'

'Okay. Thank you.'

Gwen Bailey ended the call, leaving Whitney staring at the phone. The two interactions with the parents couldn't have been more different. In her experience, reactions to bad news could vary, but she'd never been dismissed quite so quickly before. Surely the woman must have been disturbed to find out that her daughter had been dead for so long.

She left her office and went into the incident room. 'I've had confirmation that the remains found belong to Anita Bailey and Jayne Kennedy and I've just let the families know. Ellie, where are we on the files from the previous investigation?'

'They came through a while ago and I've been going through them, guv.'

'Any comments so far?'

'I don't want to say anything bad but … there's not much in there, the files are thin.'

'Remember, all those years ago things were very different, they didn't have computers to write up reports, it was done either by hand or typewriter,' Whitney said, not wanting to excuse the previous investigation but things weren't the same as they were now. 'Is there anything else you'd like to add?'

'There was some information recorded that should have been investigated but wasn't. Or if it was, they'd forgotten to write it up. A girl from St Paul's, the school the victims attended, told officers she saw Jayne and Anita speaking to a man outside the school gates at lunchtime on the day they went missing.'

'Do we have a name for this man?'

'No, we don't.' Ellie shook her head.

'A description?'

'Yes, she said he was wearing jeans and jumper, was of medium height with long, straight, brown hair to his shoulders. He had some distinguishing tattoos, one on his neck of an eagle and letters on his fingers. She wasn't sure what they spelt.'

'And this wasn't followed up?' Whitney said, tilting her head to one side.

'Not according to the files. Unless they did but forgot to write it up, as I've already said,' Ellie replied.

'Do you have the name of this girl?'

'Yes, Kathleen Fisher.'

'We need to track down both her and the man she saw with our victims.'

Whitney was astounded at the incompetence of the officers investigating the previous case. It was basic stuff they'd messed up.

'Yes, guv.'

'Was there anything else of note in the records?'

'The girls went missing during school hours. They weren't at their last lesson and nobody saw them after afternoon break on Wednesday, 7 May.'

'Finally, we're getting somewhere. Top priority is finding Kathleen Fisher. Obviously, she's now older and may have a different surname.'

'Yes, guv. I'm on to it,' Ellie said.

'I'll help,' Brian said.

Ellie glanced at Whitney and she gave a tiny nod.

'I'd rather you came with me to reinterview Anthony Gibson,' Whitney said.

'I'll grab my jacket,' Brian said, heading over to the coat stand, taking it from the hanger and shrugging it on.

As they headed out to the car park, he turned to her.

'Is there an issue with me helping Ellie? I noticed a look between the two of you.'

'Not exactly an *issue*. Ellie is streets ahead of the rest of us when it comes to technology, and it's her remit in the team. She's trained in using the self-service kiosk and is our go-to person for any research we need, especially if it's tricky. If you want to work on that side of things, then I'd rather you asked her *if* she needs help, instead of using your rank to muscle in.'

'That wasn't what I'd intended.'

'Good. I'm glad we've got that out of the way.'

They drove to the farm in relative silence and she kept taking peeps at him out of the corner of her eye. He was focused on the road ahead. Had she upset him by what she'd said about Ellie? Perhaps he wasn't used to the relaxed team atmosphere she cultivated.

When they reached the turning for the shortcut, he glanced at her. 'This way?' he said.

'It's quickest.'

'And don't forget bumpiest and dirtiest. It took me ages to clean my car after our last visit.' He scowled.

'The journey will take another ten minutes if we stick to this road. I'll leave it to you.' It was the least she could do seeing as she wasn't the one having to wash the car.

'Thanks.' He turned off his indicator and continued ahead.

When they arrived at the farm, he parked outside the front on the gravel.

'Don't forget—'

'No need. I've got it,' he said arching an eyebrow.

'Good.' She allowed herself a smile in his direction.

'Inspector.' She turned, her hand poised to knock on the front door. Anthony Gibson was heading towards them from the garage.

She didn't correct him regarding her title.

'Good morning.'

'Are you here to tell me I can resume with the work?'

'Sorry, no. We've identified the bodies found and would like to talk to you about it.'

'I can spare you five minutes as I'm due in the city for a meeting with the bank in an hour.' He stepped to the side of her and opened the front door. 'Come on through to the kitchen.'

She refrained from commenting but did catch sight of Brian suppressing a grin. He was learning fast. They would be interviewing Gibson for as long as it took. And if that meant he was late for his meeting, then so be it.

She assumed they wouldn't be offered a coffee this time and she was right, as once they arrived in the kitchen he gestured for them to sit at the table and he followed suit.

'Mr Gibson, have you heard the names Jayne Kennedy and Anita Bailey.'

'No.' He shook his head.

'They are the sixteen-year-old girls who were buried on your land. It happened in May 1980. Were you living at the farm then?'

'Yes, I was only fourteen.'

'Who else lived here at that time?'

'Only my parents. My older sister was away at university in Durham.'

'What school did you go to?' She doubted it was the one the girls attended but wanted to make sure.

'Oakford School.'

A private school ten miles out of Lenchester. So no connection.

'I'd like you to think back to that time. Someone managed to dig a big hole and bury two bodies. How would that be possible without anyone seeing?'

'If it was done during the night we wouldn't have known as the farmhouse is quite a distance from where the bodies were left and there were trees and hedges in the way.'

'What about if a car drew up? Would you have heard it, even if you didn't see the headlights?'

'It wasn't unusual for cars to come and go because of staff and their families living in the cottages, so even if we did hear a noise it wouldn't alert us to anything untoward going on.'

'We'd like a list of all the farm workers from around that time, can you get that for us?'

'I would have to ask my father.'

'Can we speak to him now?'

'He's on his way to Norwich to visit his sister, with my wife.'

'When will he be back?'

'I'm collecting him at the weekend. I'll phone this evening and ask him. We had a farm manager called Ted who lived in one of the cottages. He died about ten years ago. He was only sixty.'

'Do you know where his family are?'

'He was single.'

Damn.

'When you speak to your father please mention the girls' names and see if they mean anything to him.'

'Will do.' He glanced at his watch. 'I really need to get changed for my meeting. Is there anything else I can help you with?'

'Do you remember whether there was anything significant happening on the site around the time the girls were buried?'

'I don't recall there being anything in May of that year, but I was little more than a boy. If it was September, we used to hold an annual fayre, and in July the circus came to town, but they're the only events that I can remember.'

'Before we leave, I do have one more question. You told us that the development was a *backstop* and that, financially, you were secure. Are you sure that's the case? According to our records you've remortgaged the farm.'

His body tensed. 'It's not something I'm proud of and my father doesn't know. Once the development is completed we'll be back on an even footing. Farming isn't what it used to be.'

'A word of advice. Don't lie to the police, because it won't turn out well,' she said.

'It has nothing to do with all this, so it shouldn't matter.'

'That's for us to decide. Call the station after you've spoken to your father. Ask for me, or DS Chapman. We'll see ourselves out.'

They left and returned to Brian's car.

'You had him rattled, guv.'

'That wasn't my intention, but he shouldn't have lied. What did you make of him?'

'He was only fourteen at the time the girls were buried and didn't go to their school. I don't believe he knew anything about it. When you mentioned their names there was no recognition in his eyes.'

'I'm inclined to agree. We'll wait to hear back from him regarding his father.'

They drove back to the station and once they were in the incident room she headed over to Ellie.

'How are you getting on?'

'I've found Kathleen Fisher. Her name is now Henderson, and she lives with her husband, Dean, in Kettering, Northamptonshire. She has two grown-up children.'

'That's only forty minutes away. Thank goodness she hasn't moved to the other side of the world. Attention everyone. Ellie has tracked down Kathleen Fisher, now called Henderson. She lives in Kettering.' Whitney walked over to the board and wrote the name on there. 'I'm going to call Dr Cavendish and we'll go out to visit her.'

'Don't you want me to come with you?' Brian asked.

'No, not this time. I'm going to take George as I'd like to get her opinion on the woman. Now we know who she is, I want a thorough search done on her as she may have been involved. I also want an investigation into the school. Find names and locations of all the pupils in the missing girls' year. That should keep you busy. Brian, you can sort out who's doing what.'

Normally, she'd do it herself but as she'd refused to take him with her and, bearing in mind what George had said, she wanted to give him something to do so he felt more involved.

'Yes, guv,' he said.

She returned to her office and gave George a call.

'Where are you?' she said as soon as George answered.

'I'm at work. Where else?'

'Can you get away? We've found a witness who saw the two missing girls speaking to a man outside the school the day they disappeared. I'd like you with me when I pay her a visit.'

'What about Brian, shouldn't you be taking him?'

'Don't you start. I've already turned down his request to come with me as I want you there. The woman lives in Kettering with her husband.'

'Fine. I take it you want me to drive?'

Whitney laughed. 'Guilty as charged. So, will you come?'

'Of course. I'll pick you up in half an hour. There's something I'd like to show you.'

'What?'

'You will see soon enough,' the psychologist said as she ended the call.

Since when did George act all mysterious?

Chapter 11

Adrenaline coursed through George's veins as she opened the door to her new quartzite grey Porsche Cayenne Turbo. She'd only picked it up from the garage late yesterday afternoon and the excitement hadn't yet abated. The new car smell from the black leather interior enveloped her. There was nothing like it. Whitney called it her guilty pleasure, but that wasn't how she viewed it. There was nothing guilty about her love of cars and when she'd driven over to Ross's the previous night, she'd enjoyed putting the Porsche through its paces on the long stretches of straight road where she could put her foot down.

She hadn't mentioned to Whitney that she'd bought it. The officer had no interest in cars and couldn't understand why George did. It was an extravagance, which she wouldn't appreciate.

When she arrived at the station, she pulled into the visitors' car park and headed to the reception.

'Please could you let DCI Walker know that Dr Cavendish is here to see her,' she said to the receptionist.

After a few minutes Whitney walked out of the lift and headed towards her. She was wrapped up in a thick navy coat, knitted pink hat and matching scarf.

'Hi, George. I really must see about getting you an identification tag,' Whitney said, as they went out of the front entrance. 'Where have you parked?'

'In the visitors' car park.'

They walked around the side of the building and into the car park, which was half full.

'Where's your car?' Whitney asked, looking around and frowning.

'I've bought myself a new one, it's over there, out of the way.' George pointed to the far corner where she'd parked separate from the others as she didn't want to risk it getting damaged.

Whitney turned to her. 'So that's what you wanted to show me. I couldn't work it out. What have you got, a Ferrari? And if I'm right, don't say it's red as that would be so stereotypical of a fast car. I might even refuse to get into it.'

'No, it's not a Ferrari. It's also not red. You'll see shortly.'

They reached the car, and Whitney walked around it, her mouth open. 'You've got to be kidding me. You've bought yourself a Porsche. Bloody hell. Aren't they like hundreds of thousands of pounds?'

'I've had my eye on it for a long time. I collected it yesterday. And no, it didn't cost that much.' She wasn't going to admit the exact amount she'd paid because Whitney wouldn't understand why she'd spent so much.

'Why didn't you tell me?'

'Because it was only recently I finally made up my mind to buy it. It's not something I thought you'd have been interested in.'

She wasn't one for discussing her thought processes with anyone. She was perfectly able to make up her own mind without consulting with others. Ross had asked a similar question, as she hadn't discussed it with him either. She didn't require their input when making a decision.

'But … a Porsche. That must have cost you an arm and a leg. And some.'

'I traded my Land Rover in.'

She wasn't going to tell Whitney that money was no object. She'd had an inheritance from her grandmother many years ago, which had enabled her to buy her Victorian terraced house outright and had still left her plenty of money in the bank. She also had her university salary for day-to-day expenses. She was very comfortably off but knew that Whitney wasn't, and she didn't want to rub her nose in it.

'What did Ross say?'

'I drove over to show him last night. He liked it.'

That was an understatement. The whoops of joy Ross had made, and the way he'd run around the car like a child with a new toy, was extremely amusing. Although, when he'd asked why she hadn't consulted him at all on the purchase, she didn't give him an answer. He didn't push her for one, either. She appreciated that.

'Will you let him drive it?'

'Maybe in the future. He's not insured yet.'

She'd always been territorial over her cars. When she'd lived with Stephen, she wouldn't let him drive her car, despite him constantly asking her if he could. He'd thought he could wear her down with his nagging, but he didn't. She'd dug her heels in and wouldn't be swayed. Ross hadn't asked outright, but from his reaction to the car and his questions she suspected he would like to have the opportunity to take the wheel.

'You should insure him in case something happens, and he needs to drive it at short notice.'

Whitney had made a valid point. It wasn't something she'd considered because Ross had his own vehicle. But if they were in hers … perhaps she would insure him. Not just yet, though.

'I will give it some thought, for now I want to enjoy it myself.' She opened the door and got in.

'I'm going to enjoy it, too,' Whitney said as she slid into the passenger seat and ran her hand over it. 'Feel the leather, it's so soft. I might not be a petrolhead, like you, but even I can appreciate this luxury.' She gave a contented sigh.

'It's a hybrid, so I'm doing my bit for the environment,' she said, fastening her seat belt.

'I'd expect nothing else.' Whitney flashed a grin in her direction.

She left the car park and pulled out into oncoming traffic. After a few minutes they reached the dual carriageway and she could put her foot down. The traffic wasn't heavy, so she didn't have to stop and start.

'Have you seen Martin recently?' Whitney always asked about Ross, so she remembered to do the same.

'We text and phone regularly, but I haven't seen him for a couple of weeks. After our last case I spent some time with him in London and had a lovely time.'

'Would you say you're in a relationship?' She took her eyes off the road for a moment and glanced at Whitney.

'I don't know what you'd call it. It's certainly more than *friends with benefits* but a relationship … I'm not sure.'

'*Friends with benefits?*'

'Haven't you heard of that term? It means not in a relationship but still having the benefit of sex.'

'Interesting. What about Tiffany? Have you given her any indication you're seeing him yet?'

'No. It's not the sort of thing you can discuss when she's over the other side of the world. *Oh, by the way, I'm seeing your father.* She'd freak. I'm going to wait until she's home when we can sit down together and have a long chat about it. He wants to meet her, but if she doesn't want to meet him … I'm not going to think about it until she's back here. Whenever that's going to be.'

'But you're hoping for Christmas, although she doesn't have much time to make up her mind if she does wish to come home. Flights at this time of year are expensive, although we could contribute.'

George had given Tiffany an early twenty-first birthday present of money before she'd left for Australia. She was more than happy to help fund the flight back.

'She hasn't asked me to help financially so maybe that means she isn't going to come home after all. I've just been kidding myself. I keep thinking she's planning this massive surprise, but …' Whitney's voice tailed off. George hadn't meant to upset her.

'What about your mum and brother, have you told them about Martin?' she asked, deciding to move the subject away from Tiffany.

'I haven't mentioned him yet as I'm not sure how, or what, to tell them. He's got his work in London and I'm based here, so it's not like I can move to be with him. I'm not prepared to leave Lenchester and be away from them.'

'He could live here with you and commute to work, plenty of people do from here.'

'Stop jumping the gun. I've already said I'm not sure whether we're in a relationship, and even if we are, there are many barriers to overcome. Not least explaining to Tiffany, which is the most important.'

'But surely if you like him, she will, too.'

'Your view is too simplistic. I kept him hidden for twenty-one years, how would you feel if that had happened to you? Actually, scrap that. You're way too rational to be upset by it.' She shook her head.

'I do understand and I'm sure Tiffany will if you explain exactly what happened. Tell it to her like you told me.'

'We'll see,' Whitney said. 'Conversation over. We must nearly be there.'

George was glad to leave the subject. She hadn't realised it was going to cause such an issue.

'Yes, it's on the left.'

George pulled up outside a modern semi-detached house, with a dark blue door.

'I hope she's in. I didn't want to phone first in case it gave her time to concoct a story, or for her to tell us what she thinks we want to hear. If she's out, we'll come back later, if that's okay with you?'

'Yes, that's fine,' George said, happy for the excuse to do as much driving as possible.

They walked to the door and Whitney rang the bell. After thirty seconds she tried again, but still no reply.

'Damn. Okay, let's go,' Whitney said.

They headed back to the car and were just about to get in when a car pulled into the driveway. A woman in her fifties, with short blonde hair, rolled down the window. 'Are you here to see me?' she asked.

'We're looking for Kathleen Henderson,' Whitney said.

'That's me.'

'I'm Detective Chief Inspector Walker and this is Dr Cavendish. We'd like to come in and have a chat with you, if we may.'

'What's it about? Has something happened?' She

opened the car door and stepped out, hurrying towards them.

'Everything's fine. We'd like to talk to you about something which happened when you were at St Paul's school.'

'I left years ago, when I was sixteen. What on earth do you want to know?'

'We're investigating the disappearance of Jayne Kennedy and Anita Bailey.'

Her eyes widened. 'I've just got back from work, come on inside and we can talk there.'

She rushed past them, pulling her key out of her handbag, and they followed her down the drive, waiting while she unlocked the door and let them in. The door opened up onto a combined lounge and dining area. The room wasn't very large and was furnished sparsely, with a two-seater oat coloured sofa and a dark brown chair both facing the television in the corner which was up on the wall. The family photos mounted on the wall were the only really personal items George observed.

'Where do you work?' Whitney asked.

'I'm a part-time administrator for a firm of solicitors in town. I work mornings so I can visit my mother in the afternoons. She's in her eighties, but still lives alone, around the corner. Can I get you something to drink?'

'Coffee would be lovely, milk, no sugar,' Whitney said.

George gave a tiny smile. Some things never changed. In all the time she'd known Whitney, she'd never refused one.

'Same for me, please,' she said.

They waited while Kathleen went into the kitchen. After a few minutes she returned with three mugs on a tray which she placed on the small table. She handed one to each of them.

'When did you move from Lenchester?' Whitney asked.

'My parents moved to Kettering with my father's job, just over thirty years ago. My husband and I moved over here to be close to my mother after he died.'

'What about your family?' Whitney asked.

'I have two grown-up children. My son works in London as a dentist and my daughter lives locally with her husband and two children. I'm enjoying being a grandparent, it's so much easier than being a parent.'

'I'm sure it's fun,' Whitney said.

'What do you want to know about Anita and Jayne?' Kathleen asked.

'We've reopened the case because we now believe they didn't run away as previously thought. The remains of two bodies were recently found and they have been identified as theirs.'

Kathleen's hand shot up to her mouth. 'That's awful. So, all this time they were actually dead? Their poor families must be devastated.'

The woman's shock was certainly genuine.

'According to our records, you were interviewed at the time. Can you tell me why you were specifically singled out?' Whitney asked.

'After they'd gone missing, the police came into our class and spoke to all of form 5F together.'

'Did they speak to the other forms?' Whitney asked.

'I don't think so, but I can't be certain. We'd been together as a form from when we joined the school at thirteen, so I assume they thought we'd be the best ones to speak to. They asked if we'd seen anything that might be useful and, if so, to speak to them. I spoke up because I'd seen Anita and Jayne outside the front gate talking to a man on the day they disappeared.'

'Yes, we have that on the record. Had you seen this man before?'

'No, I hadn't, but …' She hesitated. 'I think he might have been a drug dealer.'

'What makes you say that?' Whitney asked, exchanging a quick glance with George. There had been no mention of drugs in the files.

Kathleen bit down on her bottom lip. 'I don't like to say anything bad about Jayne and Anita, especially now you've told me that they've been dead all this time. But to be honest, they weren't nice girls, they were bullies, and they picked on people. Anita was a lot worse than Jayne, but they both did it.'

'Did they pick on you?'

'Yes, they did. They would call me names because I was a bit overweight. But it's not just that they were bullies. They …' Her voice fell away.

'Go on,' Whitney said, gently.

'They used to sell drugs. The man they were with was older and had some distinctive tattoos. I thought maybe he was their dealer.'

'What sort of drugs did they sell?'

'I think it was mainly speed. I didn't buy anything from them.'

'But you knew they sold them.'

'Everybody knew.'

'The teachers, too?' George asked.

'No, obviously not.' The woman glanced at George, an incredulous expression on her face.

She acknowledged that it wasn't a well-considered question.

'You didn't mention this to the police. All you said was you saw them talking to this man and described him. Why didn't you say anything about the drugs?' Whitney asked.

'I was too scared.'

'Okay, I understand,' Whitney said. 'Is there anything else you can think of that might help with our enquiries?'

'No. It all happened so long ago, and I haven't thought about Anita and Jayne since they left.'

'Do you have any photos from your school days?'

'We weren't friends, so none including them, although come to think of it … I might have an old form photo. I'll check.'

'Thank you.'

Kathleen hurried over to the oak sideboard situated along the wall behind the dining table. She opened a drawer and pulled out an album.

'This is from when I was at school. Once Jayne and Anita had run away, our form changed for the remainder of the school year. There wasn't any bullying, and everyone was kind and friendly to each other. I still keep in touch with some people from school, even now. It's so easy with social media.' She opened the album and pulled out a photo. 'This is the school photo taken at the start of our fifth form year. That's me, and there are Jayne and Anita.' She pointed at the back row.

'I'd like to take this with me, if I may. I'll make sure it's returned to you once the investigation is over,' Whitney said.

Kathleen pulled out the photo from the album and handed it to Whitney. 'You can keep it, I have others.'

After finishing their coffee, they left the house and returned to the car.

'If only she'd spoken up sooner, the previous officers could have checked out the drug connection, and maybe the girls would still be alive,' Whitney said.

'We can't be sure, although certainly their bodies might have been found sooner. She can't be blamed, though. At sixteen she was bound to be scared of any repercussions,' George said.

'True, although there's not a lot of point in going over that. But we do have a potential motive. Maybe the girls ripped off their drug dealer or did something that upset him enough to cause him to murder them. How did you rate Kathleen Henderson? Was she telling the truth? Was she hiding anything?'

'There was nothing in her manner, or the way in which she spoke to us to indicate she wasn't telling the truth. I don't believe she was hiding anything from us, either. And her shock at finding out they'd been dead for all that time was evident, in the way she stiffened involuntarily, and her hand shot up to her mouth.'

'That's good to know. Let's go back to the station and get the team on to it.'

'I've got to go back to work, so I'll drop you off there.'

'That's fine. I need to see the super as she wants to be kept up to date on the investigation.'

'How's your relationship with her going?'

'It's early days, and this is our first case together, so I'm reserving judgement. So far, so good. She certainly seemed okay when we had our initial chat, but she's no pushover. She wants to be kept in the loop, but I can live with that if she treats me fairly and not like Jamieson did.'

'Let's hope so.' Although knowing Whitney as she did, she anticipated there would be some issues.

George wasn't totally convinced it was only males the officer had issues with. She believed it could be authority figures in general. They would find out soon enough if Whitney did something her new super didn't agree with.

Chapter 12

The new super's office was on the floor below Whitney's, so she took the stairs. On the door, in gold lettering, was the name *Detective Superintendent Clyde*. She knocked and waited.

'Come in.'

'I'm here to give you an update on the case, ma'am,' Whitney said as she stood in the doorway.

'Good to see you, Whitney.' Clyde smiled and gestured for her to enter. 'Take a seat.' She indicated for Whitney to sit in front of her desk.

On the wall behind where the super sat there were no certificates from Oxford University, like Jamieson used to have for everybody to see, but instead a nice painting of a country scene.

'Ma'am, we've just returned from visiting—'

'One moment,' Clyde said, interrupting. 'First, I want to know how everything's going with the new team.'

'Three of the team I know well, as you're aware, and the other two seem to be settling in. Obviously, it's going to take time for us all to gel, and get used to working in different ways, but I have high hopes for it being a success.'

'We're lucky to have recruited Brian Chapman. He was highly thought of at Willsden, and there were others here who wanted him on their team, DCI Masters for one. Did you know Chapman trained at the Met?'

She'd reserve judgement on the *lucky* bit as they hadn't worked together long enough.

'Yes, ma'am, he has informed us of that on several occasions.' Damn, she hadn't meant it to sound like that.

'Is there an issue?' the super asked, her eyes locking with Whitney.

Clearly nothing got past her. Whitney would have to be mindful of that.

'No, not at all. Sorry, I didn't mean it to sound like that, he's already proving his worth.'

'Good. Chapman only moved for family issues, otherwise, he would probably still be in London. Keep an eye on him, he should be due to take his Inspectors' exam soon. We want to make sure he has a good experience here so we can hang on to him. I was part of his interview panel and was extremely impressed. So, I repeat, we're very lucky to have him.'

'Yes, ma'am. Back to the case, we've identified the remains as belonging to two teenage girls, Anita Bailey and Jayne Kennedy. They were classed as runaways when they went missing in 1980. Unfortunately, the investigation wasn't run as tightly as it should have been, or they might have been found sooner.'

'Please explain.'

'We interviewed a woman who was at school with them. She'd actually seen the girls talking to an older man outside the school gates on the day they disappeared. She did report it, but it wasn't followed up. She believed the man might have been a drug dealer as the girls were known for selling drugs at school.'

'And none of this was recorded?' the super frowned.

'No, although in the officers' defence, the woman didn't mention they were selling drugs because she was too scared of any repercussions.'

'At age sixteen that's understandable. But you're right, the sighting of the girls with this man should have been pursued further. What are your next steps?'

'I'll ask Ellie, Constable Naylor, to investigate. If anyone can find this drug dealer it's her. We know he had a distinguishing tattoo on his neck and others on his hands.'

'We need to be mindful of the resource implications, in respect of the time allowed to investigate this case, as it dates back so many years ago. We'll give it two weeks, and then reassess as we may have other, more pressing, cases. I will arrange a press conference as we need the public's input. I don't know how you ran them with Superintendent Jamieson, but I do like mine to run in a specific fashion,' she said.

'Yes, ma'am.'

'I will be doing the speaking and you will be there as support if I need you.'

Whitney bit back a smile. The super operated in a similar way to her, it was good to find something they had in common. It was certainly different from Jamieson, who couldn't hand over to her quickly enough if he'd believed something was getting too tricky and there was the possibility that he could look ineffective.

'Yes, ma'am. Understood.'

'I'll let you know when I've arranged it, which I'm hoping might be later today.'

'Yes, ma'am. Whenever you're ready is fine. Is that all, as I do need to get back to speak to DC Naylor.'

Clyde couldn't quite meet her eyes. What was going on? Surely, they didn't have a problem already.

'One more thing.' And here it was. 'I'm not sure how you're going to take this, but it shouldn't be an issue.'

Whitney frowned. She didn't like the sound of this. 'What is it?'

'I've just been informed that Chief Superintendent Douglas is being transferred to the Lenchester force.'

'You're kidding?' she blurted out, clenching her fists and banging them on her legs.

The one person in the whole world who she never wanted to see again was going to be around. All the bloody time.

'Now, Whitney,' Clyde said calmly. 'This isn't going to affect you because he's going to be my immediate boss, not yours. I know you've had issues in the past, but he won't be interfering in the running of your team, I can promise you that.'

'If you say so, ma'am.'

'I'd like to know exactly why you have a problem with him.'

Should she tell her? At least if she did, then she would know and hopefully understand. It wouldn't change the fact he was now going to be around, but it might ease the pressure.

'I don't wish this to go any further, ma'am.'

'This is between you and me.' The super leant back in her chair and gave Whitney her full attention.

'When I joined the force over twenty years ago, Douglas, sorry, I mean Chief Superintendent Douglas, was a sergeant. He tried it on with me and I refused. I told him, in no uncertain terms that if he ever did anything like that again, I'd make him pay. He left me alone after that but ever since he's had it in for me and, whenever he's had the opportunity, he's tried to derail my career.'

'But he hasn't succeeded.'

'That's a matter of opinion. There was one incident when I should have been promoted to inspector, but I missed out on that because of him. As it turned out, it didn't matter, and I was promoted a few months later. That happened about eleven years ago.'

'Has anything else occurred between the two of you?'

She might as well tell the super everything, so she could see what an arse Douglas was.

'He did try to interfere in one of the investigations last year when two of his officers from the Regional Force were in Lenchester working with us on a case. He wanted me removed from the investigation, stating that I wasn't doing my job properly, but Superintendent Jamieson dealt with it, after which time he left me alone.'

Clyde sighed and shook her head. 'If there are any incidents you come to me. Any at all, however small they might be. I don't want you attempting to deal with them yourself.'

The super was going to support her. Whitney nodded her approval, but she wasn't convinced that Douglas would leave her alone.

'Yes, ma'am. I appreciate your response.'

'Thank you for being honest with me, Whitney. I'll make sure that nothing happens to undermine you, but I do expect you to show him the level of respect his position deserves.'

'Of course, ma'am,' she said, crossing her fingers behind her back. Childish, she knew, but she couldn't help it.

'I'll let you know about the press conference once it's been arranged,' the super said.

Whitney kept it together until she was away from the office. Her mind was whirring. What the bloody hell had she done to deserve Douglas being back? Whatever Clyde said, she knew that he'd be out to get her. He'd find a way. She'd have to leave, what else could she do?

She marched along the corridor, up the stairs and into her office, slamming the door behind her. She needed to speak to Ellie immediately, but had to calm down first. She pulled out her phone and hit speed dial for George.

'Hello, Whitney,' her friend said, answering after the first ring.

'You're never going to believe what's happened. It's ridiculous. I'm going to have to leave. There's nothing else for me to do. I'm—'

'Whitney,' George interrupted sharply. 'Take a breath and tell me what's happened.'

'I've just been in with the super…' She exhaled a long breath.

'Is it something she said?'

'No. She was fine and I'm happy with how that's going. But … I can hardly bring myself to say it … She told me that Dickhead Douglas has been transferred to Lenchester. He's Chief Superintendent. Her boss.' There was silence at the end of the line. 'Well, say something.'

'Does she know what happened between the two of you?'

'Yes, I told her everything and she said she'd look out for me. But talk's cheap, you've witnessed first-hand how devious Dickhead can be.'

'If she said she will make sure it's okay and he's not your immediate superior, I think it might be fine.'

'What do you mean it *might* be fine? Look what he did before when we were working with Vic and Terry from the Regional Force. If it wasn't for Jamieson, he would have succeeded in getting me removed from the case. He's always there trying to sabotage my career.'

'But he wasn't successful because your immediate superior officer made sure it didn't happen. Whatever you thought of Jamieson, he actually did stick up for you, if you remember.'

'Yes, I do remember. I admit that Jamieson is a better option than Douglas because he didn't do anything behind my back, he was upfront about it. Douglas, on the other hand, was a devious little shit. It's crazy and I'm going to have to look over my shoulder all the time.'

'You don't know that. You're pre-empting what might happen. You always do a good job, and there's no reason for that to change. Douglas will have more important things to worry about than trying to ruin your career. You really need to get some perspective on this. The success of your career doesn't hang on Douglas's shoulders.'

'I wish I had your confidence, because at the moment I don't know what to do,' she said.

'Try not to think about him. Compartmentalise.'

'Yes, yes, yes. Compartmentalise. Here you go again. I'll try my hardest, but I'm not you and I'm not sure it's going to work.'

'You have to make it work or your life will be a misery. You enjoy your job. You believe your new super is going to work out. Concentrate on that relationship and take it one day at a time.'

What she'd give for even a quarter of George's rationality at the moment.

'Yes, you're right. I'm sorry, I just needed to let off steam and get it out of my system. I'll say goodbye now as I've got to speak to the team. We need to find out who this drug dealer is pronto. We've only got two weeks on the case before the super wants to move us onto something else. I'll let you know how we go, because once we have him, I'm going to want you in the interview.'

'No problem. I'll wait to hear from you. And don't worry, it will be fine.'

'Are you jinxing again?

'No. Stop with the bloody jinxing,' George said.

Whitney grinned, and ended the call. She then went into the incident room and over to Ellie's desk.

'The man with the tattoos who Kathleen Henderson saw, we believe could be a drug dealer. Knowing that should help you track him down.'

'Okay, guv,' Ellie said.

'Attention, everyone. I've just come back from interviewing the woman who saw the two victims talking with the man outside the school gates. We've learnt that the girls were selling drugs, and it's possible the man they were talking to was a drug dealer.'

'Nothing was said about this before,' Brian said. 'Is she telling the truth?'

'Yes, I believe so. She was too scared to say anything to the police at the time she was interviewed but now we know, we should be able to identify this man. The super's arranging a press conference for later today which will help move the investigation forward.'

Chapter 13

Whitney brushed her hair and smeared on some lip gloss so she looked presentable for the press conference. After she double-checked herself in the small hand mirror she kept in her drawer, she left for Clyde's office.

The door was slightly ajar, and she tapped and stuck her head around.

The super was standing by the window, looking extremely tall in her uniform. Why hadn't Whitney put on heels, so she wouldn't look so short next to her? Because they weren't practical for work, and that's what counted. That didn't stop her from standing a little straighter as she entered the room, though.

'I'm ready for the press conference, ma'am.'

Clyde looked at her watch. 'We've got fifteen minutes to go, time to go over everything we have so far.'

Whitney stood by one of the chairs and leant against it. 'The victims were selling drugs to their fellow students and we believe the man at the school gates could have been their drug dealer. We're not certain yet, but we're researching into it. Nothing has changed since earlier when we discussed it.'

'I will be letting the media know the names of the girls and where they were found.'

'We don't usually release names straightaway, ma'am,' Whitney said.

It had been Lenchester's policy since before Whitney started working there and, although it was different from other forces, it worked for them. It wasn't done to keep the public in the dark, but more that they'd found they were able to move forward quicker on investigations by operating the policy.

'As these deaths were from decades ago and we're asking people to remember them, we have no choice.'

She made a good point, not to mention it was her decision, whatever Whitney's opinion.

'Obviously, it's going to alert the killer, or killers, to the fact that we're looking for them too, assuming they're still alive.'

If the culprits were no longer around it would make their job impossible and meant they'd got away with their crimes.

'That's a risk we have to take. It's one of the problems of investigating cold cases.'

'As you wish,' she said, wincing as her words were delivered with unintentional sarcasm.

'Yes, it is as I wish, Whitney.' Clyde looked down at her from under her eyelashes and she squirmed.

She really shouldn't underestimate her new boss.

'Yes, ma'am.'

'If that's all, I think we'll be going down. Who's the person in PR that we'll be meeting? I forgot to ask my assistant after she arranged it.'

'In the past, it's always been Melissa, but I'm not sure if she's still here after the upheaval.'

'We'll soon find out. Let's go,' Clyde said, as she smoothed down her skirt and then strode past Whitney.

They took the lift to the ground floor and headed to the new purpose-built conference room. When they arrived, Melissa was standing outside.

'Hello, Melissa,' she said, smiling. 'This is Detective Superintendent Clyde.'

'Nice to meet you,' the PR officer said. 'This new room is bigger than the one we had previously. Cameras and reporters are separated, rather than mics being at the back dangling over everyone. We're full already and you'll recognise all the same faces,' she said to Whitney.

'Some of them have been coming in for years,' Whitney said to Clyde. 'We know them well and they're not a bad bunch … for press.'

'Good. Lead the way, Melissa,' Clyde said, and they followed her in. Instead of having a table, as they had in the past, there was a podium. Melissa stepped onto it and stood behind the lectern while Whitney and Clyde stood to one side.

'Good afternoon, everybody. Thank you for coming in to our first press conference in the new building.' The voices hushed and everyone stared in Melissa's direction. 'I'm pleased to see so many familiar faces. I'd like to introduce you to Detective Superintendent Clyde who will be briefing you today.'

The PR officer stepped down and Clyde took her place. She didn't just go rushing in but took her time and scanned the room. Had she had theatrical training? She was very impressive. Whitney could learn a lot from her.

'Good afternoon. I'm Detective Superintendent Clyde. I'm new to the area and as yet do not recognise any of you, although I've been assured by Detective Chief Inspector Walker that most of you have been coming here for years and we have a good relationship with you. I hope that this will continue.' She paused while there was chatter between the reporters. 'I'm here today to report the discovery of the buried remains of two sixteen-year-old girls.' The noise level spiked from chattering voices, as usually occurred when young people were involved. 'These bodies had been buried since 1980.'

'They've only just been found?' a reporter in the front row called out.

'That is correct. They were discovered on Oak Tree Farm after digging started for the new housing development.'

'Can you give us more information?' a reporter who Whitney didn't recognise called out.

'We've identified the young women as Jayne Kennedy and Anita Bailey, ex-pupils of St Paul's school. They were reported as missing on 7 May 1980 after not returning home from school that afternoon.'

Whitney scanned the room. Notes were being furiously scribbled, and phones held out to capture everything being said by the super.

'I remember that case,' an older reporter sitting close to the podium said. 'The parents insisted that they hadn't taken off and put posters up everywhere. We reported on it.'

'At the time they were believed to have been runaways and no further action was taken in order to locate them,' the super said.

'Are you saying the police made a mistake? That they should have listened to the parents instead of insisting the girls had left of their own accord?' the reporter continued.

'No, I am not. That would be extremely presumptuous,' Clyde said. 'The victims' bodies have been discovered and we would like anybody who may have information that could help with the investigation to get in touch with us. All contact will be treated in confidence. Any questions?'

The super's no-nonsense manner was impressive.

'Is it possible that someone put the bodies there to stop the development?' A woman on the left said.

'We're not ruling out anything at this stage, although the post-mortems haven't indicated that the bodies were placed there recently,' Clyde said.

The super fielded several more questions and then ended the conference.

'I think that went well,' Clyde said to Whitney as they left the room and Melissa went on ahead.

'Yes, ma'am. Interesting question regarding whether the bodies were moved there just to stop the development. It isn't something we'd considered,' Whitney said.

'It seems unlikely as the forensic examination of the bodies and the surrounding soil would have indicated it.'

'Of course,' she agreed.

They walked to the lift and got in. Whitney pressed the button for the fourth floor for the super and the fifth for herself.

'Keep me informed of anything that happens. I'm not sure whether we'll get any phone calls, but it's certainly worth a try.'

'Yes, ma'am. I should soon have more for you on the man who was seen by the school gates.'

'Excellent. Good work, Whitney, keep it up,' the super said, as the lift door opened on her floor and she stepped out.

The doors closed, leaving Whitney feeling like a child being praised by a teacher. But if that was her way of working, she'd get used to it. After getting out of the lift on her floor she headed down the corridor. She pushed open the door to the incident room and walked in to see how they were getting on.

'We've just had the press conference. I'm not sure if it's going to bring anything useful, but we do need to make sure someone is here to answer the phone.'

'I can,' Meena said. 'My husband's working this evening so it'll give me something to do.'

'Thank you. I don't want you staying after ten, any calls after that can go to voicemail. Brian, where are we on contacting pupils from the school?'

'I have Doug, Frank and Meena working on tracing both pupils and teachers. They're going through the list and contacting them. So far, nothing has come up. I have heard from Anthony Gibson, though.'

'I thought he wasn't speaking to his dad until this evening.'

'He called sooner. The father didn't know the girls, nor did he remember anything significant happening around that time. He'd confirmed his son's recollection of the farm manager working there and said, that other than him there were three farmhands at the time, none of them are still working there.'

'Did he give you their names?'

'Only first names, guv. Alf, Bert and Wayne. But we'll find them.'

'Good. Ellie, do you have anything?'

'Yes, guv,' Ellie said. 'I checked the records for anyone arrested around the time in relation to possession of drugs, or dealing, and then looked through their photos and found a man with the neck tattoo mentioned by Kathleen Henderson in her statement. He's Reginald Shaw, who's in his late sixties, and is currently inside. I'm certain he's the man who was with the victims outside the school.'

'What's he in prison for?'

'Double murder. It was a robbery gone wrong and he's done fifteen years, so far. He was given two consecutive life sentences.'

'What else do we know about him?'

'He lived in Parkway, and is married, with a daughter aged forty-three. His police record goes back for decades. He has a long history of offences, mainly petty, and has been in and out of prison. The murders were his first recorded offences of that level.'

'Any drug offences?'

'Possession only, not dealing, and that was thirty years ago.'

'Brian, take Doug and reinterview Kathleen Henderson. Take a photo of Shaw and confirm that he's the man she saw. It is many years later, but she might still recognise him, especially in respect of the tattoos. Text me once you know and I'll arrange a visit to the prison tomorrow, but it's pointless doing so until we know he's the one. How long has Shaw been married, Ellie?'

'Forty-four years.'

'That means his wife would have been around at the time of the girls' disappearance. Once we have confirmation that Shaw is our man I want you to interview her, Brian. Find out what she knows.'

'Today?' he asked.

'Tomorrow's fine, Ellie will give you the address.'

'Okay, guv.'

'Let's go over what we're all going to be doing. Meena, you're staying to answer the phones to see if anything useful comes in. Brian, you and Doug will visit Kathleen

Henderson and if he's our man, tomorrow you'll visit Shaw's wife.'

'What about me?' Frank asked.

'I want you to help Ellie.'

'Have you heard the rumour, guv?' Frank said, just as she'd turned to go back to her office.

'What rumour?' Doug said as he was half out the door, following Brian.

'Who's coming back to work here.'

Damn. How did they get to hear so quickly?

'I've heard nothing,' Doug said.

'That's because you don't know the right people.'

'And you do, I suppose. Come on, spill,' Doug said.

Frank looked at her. 'Guv?'

'Yes, I do know who you're referring to and, yes, it's true,' she said, trying to keep the emotion from her voice.

'Who is it?' Doug demanded.

'Dick—'

'Frank,' Whitney snapped, giving him a warning look. She didn't want the nickname to be known to Brian and Meena.

'Detective Superintendent Douglas,' Frank, replied a smirk on his face.

'Chief Superintendent,' Whitney corrected.

'Oh ...' Frank said.

'That's enough with the gossip.' She turned and marched to her office.

Maybe she'd talk to Frank, Doug and Ellie separately and warn them about discussing Douglas and, in particular, her nickname for him, in front of Brian and Meena. It was tricky as Brian was their superior officer, but she knew the officers well enough to trust them not to make things difficult for her.

She hadn't gone out of her way to tell the team the

nickname she'd given him, but when they were working on the *Carriage Killer* case with two of the Regional Force detectives and Douglas interfered, they'd overheard her referring to him as such. It had been a source of amusement to the team, especially when they were socialising, away from the office.

She sat behind her desk and pulled out her phone to call George.

'It's me,' she said when George answered. 'We've almost certainly identified the man waiting outside the gates of the school, he's currently inside for murder.'

'Interesting,' George said.

'Yes, that's what I thought. Once I've got confirmation it's him I'm going to arrange for us to visit him tomorrow. I'm hoping you can come with me, as I've already given Brian something else to do.'

'Yes, I'm available. What time should I pick you up?'

'I'll let you know once it's confirmed.'

Chapter 14

George sat in her car in the visitors' car park, strumming her fingers on the steering wheel. Where was Whitney? She'd been waiting for ten minutes already. There wasn't even a pleasant view to occupy her as the new station was on the edge of the city and part of an industrial area.

Five minutes later, when George was just about to pick up the phone and call, Whitney arrived and hitched herself up into the car.

'Why is it that all car manufacturers assume anyone getting into a four-wheel-drive car is tall? It's most annoying.' She wriggled into the seat. 'Sorry, I'm late. The time got away from me.'

Where are we heading?'

'Brentwood Prison in Nottingham.'

A long drive. That pleased her immediately.

'I know the place, it's just off the motorway.'

'We're lucky we've managed to secure an interview with Shaw so quickly because these places can be a law unto themselves sometimes.'

'Did the press conference produce anything?'

'According to Meena, who worked on the phones until ten last night, we've had various sightings of the girls in 1980, in places all over the country. Nothing useful so far, but she's following up anything that comes through. I also had confirmation last night from Brian that Shaw was the man Kathleen Henderson saw talking to the girls.'

'I assumed that had been the case, or you would have cancelled our visit today.'

'True.' Whitney stroked the dashboard. 'I still can't get used to this new car of yours. How are you enjoying it?'

'I wish I'd bought it sooner. It's responsive, grips well, and accelerates like a dream,' she said, turning to face Whitney and smiling.

'You're such a petrolhead.'

'You're absolutely right.' She sucked in a contented breath, started the engine and headed out of the car park.

The drive to the prison took just over forty minutes, and the motorway stretch was particularly enjoyable as she was able to put her foot down.

'This isn't an old prison, by the looks of it,' George said, as they arrived.

From the outside it looked like several large three-storey warehouses, with tiny windows every few metres.

'It was built ten years ago. It's classed as a category C, which is for those who aren't eligible for an open prison but are unlikely to try to escape.'

'If Shaw's been incarcerated for murder, wouldn't that make him a maximum-security prisoner?'

'They must have assessed him as being suitable for being housed here. Remember, he's in his late sixties so it's not like he'd be able to scale the walls and make a dash for it.'

After passing through the barrier, they went into the entrance and signed themselves in. They were escorted to a small room with a light wooden table and four plastic chairs, two either side.

Shaw was already in there, seated behind the table wearing handcuffs, his hands resting on the table. He was small, with a pale, gaunt face. His hair was fine and grey, and what little he had left was cut short. Despite having faded, the tattoo of an eagle on his neck was still evident. He had *LOVE* and *HATE* tattooed across his fingers. Those, too, had faded.

When they walked in, he looked at them, the expression on his face blank. Genuine or fake. She would soon find out.

Whitney turned to the officer who was with them. 'You can wait outside.' He left, and they sat down opposite Shaw. 'Hello, Reg. My name's Detective Chief Inspector Walker and this is Dr Cavendish, she's a forensic psychologist. We've come to speak to you about some murders that took place in 1980.' He eyed them suspiciously but remained silent. 'They were sixteen-year-old girls and their names were Anita Bailey and Jayne Kennedy.'

His eyes flickered, becoming more alert. 'You can't pin it on me,' he said, his voice gravelly.

'Nobody said we were. You were one of the last people to have seen the girls alive, talking to them outside the gates at St Paul's school on 7 May 1980. What was your conversation about?'

'Errr … that's a long time ago,' he said, glancing up as if he was trying to remember.

His attempt to act blasé was in fact telling her the complete opposite. He knew exactly what Whitney was talking about.

'Yes,' Whitney said.

'I dunno,' he said shrugging.

'You were identified by a student from the school. She

saw you talking to Jayne and Anita. Do you admit to being there at the time?'

'Yeah. Maybe. I can't remember. I was probably off my head on something.'

'The witness didn't say you looked out of it,' Whitney said.

'How the fuck would they know?' He stared directly at them.

'Do you admit to knowing Anita Bailey and Jayne Kennedy?' Whitney asked.

'That depends.' He leant back in his chair, a self-satisfied expression on his face. 'I might suddenly remember something, if it's worth it.'

'I'm not in a position to be able to authorise anything,' Whitney said, her voice flat.

Every criminal thought they had a right to bargain. It was extremely frustrating and annoyed Whitney immensely. She blamed it on all the police dramas on TV.

'I want out of here to see my family before it's too late.' His eyes glazed over.

Something was upsetting him.

'Before what's too late?' Whitney asked.

'My wife's got cancer. She's dying and I want to be with her.'

'I can't offer you a deal, that only happens on TV, but if you're up for parole, I can let the board know you've helped us,' Whitney said.

'It's not enough.' He shook his head.

'It's all I can offer, and it's better than nothing,' Whitney said.

He was silent for a while, staring at them both. 'Okay. I'll tell you what I know. But you'd better put in a good word for me.' He sat upright in his chair, resting his arms on the table.

'Do you remember Anita and Jayne?' Whitney asked, as she pulled out a notepad and pen from her pocket and put them on the table in front of her.

'What's that for?' He nodded at them.

'To record your answers to my questions?'

'Like a statement?' He clenched his fists.

'No. It's not a statement. It's a record of our conversation for my use only.'

'Well it better not be, because I'm not signing nothing.'

'Understood. Now, let's get back to my question. Anita and Jayne, what can you tell me about them?'

'Before I say anything, I want you to promise that you're not going to do me because of their age.' His eyes darted from Whitney to George.

'For goodness sake, we're talking decades ago so, unless you were involved in their deaths, then the statute of limitations has passed. Our sole aim is to identify who killed them and you might be in possession of some vital information.'

George nudged Whitney with her foot. Getting riled wasn't going to work if they wanted to learn more about the girls. Shaw had the upper hand, whether he realised it or not.

'I had nothing to do with their deaths, before you start accusing me.'

Nothing on his face led her to think otherwise.

'Duly noted,' Whitney replied, her voice much calmer. 'Now tell me about the girls and your connection with them.'

'They were selling for me at the school. It was a nice little earner for all of us.'

'What did they sell?' Whitney asked.

'Speed and weed, not the hard stuff.'

'When you met the girls the day they went missing, what did you talk about?'

'I wasn't lying before. I can't remember.' He pulled his arms in towards his body.

Classic lying behaviour.

'After they disappeared, did you wonder where they were? Did you try to contact them?'

'I don't remember.'

He remained unnaturally still, and she nudged Whitney gently with her foot to let her know that, in her opinion, he wasn't telling the truth.

'I don't believe you,' Whitney said. 'If you're not prepared to be honest with me, then you can forget me putting in a good word to the parole board.'

'It's the truth,' he insisted.

'Last chance. If you don't want to tell me what you were talking about, then tell me what you did *after* your meeting with Anita and Jayne.'

'I was with another kid from their school. A boy … now I remember.' He tilted his head to one side. 'I didn't see them again because this boy started selling for me. He was better than them. The girls were a right pain in the arse, and I didn't trust them.'

'Suddenly, you're remembering all of this,' Whitney said, arching an eyebrow.

'At my age the memory isn't great.' He tapped the side of his head.

'How long were you with this boy?' Whitney asked, jotting down some notes.

'All afternoon, then I went home to the missus.'

'What's the name of this boy?'

'Nigel.'

'Do you know his last name?' Whitney asked.

'No. But you'll find him with a name like *Nigel*. He went to St Paul's.'

'How old was he when he worked for you?' Whitney asked.

'No idea. Fifteen or sixteen, maybe.'

'And he'll be able to vouch for you?'

'If he remembers.'

'How long did this Nigel sell drugs for you?'

'Not long. I got done for robbery and went inside for two years. I stopped dealing when I came out.' He paused. 'For a while.'

'Did you contact Nigel after your release?'

'No.' He folded his arms across his chest. 'That's it. You get no more from me. Are you going to help me get out of here so I can see my wife?'

'We'll be checking your story once we've found this Nigel. Then we'll be in touch.'

'Make sure you do.'

They left the interview room and the prison. Once they were in the car Whitney turned to her.

'What do you think, was he telling the truth?' Whitney said.

'Eventually.'

'Do you think he was responsible for their deaths?'

'His body language didn't indicate he was, but you would still need to confirm it.'

'I'll get Ellie to track down the student he said he was with, and we'll interview him.'

Chapter 15

Whitney was sitting at her desk with George peering over her shoulder, while they read the pathology report from Claire and Leon. The date of deaths were recorded as 7 May 1980 as that was the day the girls were last seen, and there were no scientific tests available which could be more precise.

She glanced up and saw Ellie heading towards them. She beckoned for her to come in.

'Guv, I've found Nigel Young. He was the only Nigel in the school at that time, which made him easy to locate.'

'Excellent. Any chance he lives close by?'

'Yes. He's in Great Underwood.'

Whitney knew the village. It was twenty miles north of Lenchester. 'What else did you discover?'

'He's married with a family and is an optometrist. He has his own practice in the city. I've checked and it's open until five.'

'Okay, we'll go out to see him now. Thanks, Ellie.'

After the officer had left, Whitney grabbed her coat

from the peg on the back of her door and headed into the incident room, with George following.

As they got in there, Brian walked in with Doug.

'I'm glad to have caught you, guv,' he said, as he approached them. 'We've visited the house where Shaw's wife lives, but she wasn't there. I thought we'd try again in a little while.'

'According to Shaw she has cancer so when you do see her, be gentle.'

'Will do.'

'Dr Cavendish and I are heading out to see Nigel Young, who Shaw said he was with for the rest of the afternoon after he'd spoken to the girls. Young is another ex-student from St Paul's and he's now an optometrist in Lenchester.'

'He goes from hanging out with drug dealers to becoming a professional person. That's novel,' Brian said, arching an eyebrow.

'But not unheard of. We'll find out more when we see him. He's also a potential suspect.'

'You think it was him and Shaw?'

'It's a possibility. When you speak to Shaw's wife, ask if she remembers the girls and Nigel Young.'

'Okay, guv. I'll also find out if she can vouch for Shaw later in the afternoon after he left Young, though that's a long shot after all that time.'

'A long shot, plus we don't know the exact time they died. But it's still worth asking, she might provide us with some useful information. We'll see you later.'

They left the station and drove into the city centre to Nigel Young's practice. It was a flashy showroom selling expensive designer glasses. He must be doing well for himself.

'Hello,' Whitney said to the woman behind the reception desk. 'I'm Detective Chief Inspector Walker and this is Dr Cavendish. We're here to see Nigel Young.'

'He's in the middle of an eye examination and can't be disturbed.'

'How long will it take?' Whitney asked.

'It shouldn't be much longer, but he does have an appointment straight after.'

'He'll have to see us first.'

They walked away from the desk and she stared at the rows of frames.

'I hate to admit it, but I'm going to need reading glasses soon. I can't see as well as I used to,' Whitney said.

'That's your age,' George said.

'Thank you very much, you really know how to make a girl feel good about herself,' she said, giving a wry smile.

'It's true. Our eyesight deteriorates as we get older. You're no different from anyone else, so no need to feel bad about it.' George leant in and picked up a pair of oval frames and held them in front of her. 'These will suit the shape of your face, why don't you try them.'

As Whitney took them, she glanced at the price. 'What? Four hundred pounds? I think I'll pick up some cheap magnifying glasses from the chemist the next time I'm passing.'

'They're not very good for you as—'

A door to the rear of the reception opened, and a man came out. After he'd paid, the receptionist scurried into the room he'd been in. She returned in less than a minute.

'Mr Young can see you now.'

'Thank you,' Whitney said as they walked past her.

As they entered the examination room, a tall man with dark hair streaked with grey, stood.

'Has something happened to my family?' he asked, the

lines around his eyes tight. 'My receptionist should have interrupted.'

'We're not here about your family. 'We're investigating the deaths of two sixteen-year-old girls whose bodies were recently found at Oak Tree Farm,' Whitney said, closing the door behind them.

'Yes, I know the deaths you're referring to, I saw them reported on the news.'

'Do you remember Anita Bailey and Jayne Kennedy?'

'They went to my school, but we weren't friends.'

'They disappeared on the 7 May 1980. What can you tell me about that day?'

'That day?' he replied frowning. 'I'm sorry, I have no recollection of my movements all those years ago. My memory is shocking, as my wife will confirm. In fact, I can barely remember what we had for dinner last night.' He gave that *I'm just a helpless man* shrug, that she believed some women found attractive, but it drove her mad.

'Perhaps I can help jog your memory. Earlier we interviewed Reginald Shaw and he informed us that you were together during the afternoon of that day.'

The colour leached from his face and he dropped down on his chair, his hands fidgeting in his lap. Whitney and George took a seat opposite.

'Look,' Young said, leaning forward and staring at her intently. 'The time you're referring to is a part of my life that I have buried. Nobody knows about my past, especially that I was connected to Shaw. A drug dealer and murderer.'

'So you admit to selling drugs for him at school?' Whitney asked, pulling out her notepad and pen from her pocket and making some notes.

'Yes.'

'And you took over from Jayne and Anita, who worked for him previously?'

'Yes, they'd gone to work for another dealer. From what I remember he'd given them a bigger cut.'

'How did Shaw react when they left him?' Whitney asked.

'He wasn't happy about it. He …' His voice tailed off.

'He did what?' Whitney asked, locking eyes with him.

'As I remember, he made some threats.'

'What sort of threats?' Whitney asked.

'He said he'd make sure they wouldn't make any money, that we would have all the drugs business in the school and they'd be left with nothing.'

'Did he threaten to physically harm them?'

'Not that I remember.'

'When he spoke to Anita and Jayne outside the gates on the day they went missing, could they have been having an argument about them leaving him?'

'Yes, that's entirely possible. I wasn't there, but in the afternoon, he wasn't happy because he was the one who'd recruited them in the first place.'

'Do you know the name of the new dealer they started working for?'

'No, I don't. Shaw will, though.'

'I'm curious about there being *two* drug dealers supplying the school. There must have been a lot of drug-taking going on. Was there enough for both dealers to make a profit?'

'It wasn't like the drug operations of today. Kids took pills and smoked weed, but not large quantities and the dealers' operations weren't huge. From what I remember Shaw telling me, it was a sideline.'

'It must have helped your business when the girls *disappeared*.' Whitney locked eyes with him. He didn't look away.

'A little.' He paused. 'But … surely you're not suggesting that I had anything to do with it? I didn't. You have to believe me. I knew nothing about what happened to them.' His eyes darted from Whitney to George. Panic etched across his face.

He wasn't coming across as guilty.

'We're investigating all avenues. According to Shaw, on that afternoon you were together. Is that the case?'

'It's very likely, as there was a time when I regularly skipped school and would spend time with him. We'd go and play snooker or sit in a pub. I'm not proud of my behaviour and what I got up to, but that's all in the past. As you can see,' he gestured to his examination room. 'I managed to get my life back together. I left school at sixteen and worked in a shop for several years. When I was twenty, I enrolled at college and studied for my A levels, then went on to university and became an optometrist. But, as I've already told you, my family knows nothing of this. They'd be appalled if they found out.'

'Mr Young, anything you tell us will be treated as confidential, but we do need to solve these murders. Jayne and Anita were only sixteen. Whatever they did, they didn't deserve to die.'

'I understand.' He bowed his head.

'You said it was *very likely* that you were with Shaw on the7th of May. Can you be more specific?'

'I don't remember exact days from all those years ago, but if he said he was with me, then I'm inclined to believe him.'

That would hardly stand up in court.

'Returning to the threats Shaw made against the girls, were they on the day that they went missing?' George asked.

'Maybe. I'm not sure. It could have been. Yes.'

'Only a moment ago, you weren't one hundred per cent certain that you were with Shaw on the 7th of May, yet now you're remembering his mood after seeing the girls. Why is that?'

'The more we're talking, the more it's coming back to me. That's all,' Young said. 'You should know, it's how the memory works.'

'Is there anything else you can think of that might help us in our enquiry into the girls' deaths? Do you know of anyone who had a grudge against them, other than Shaw?' Whitney asked.

'No. I hardly knew the girls.'

'Did you buy drugs from them before you started selling for Shaw?'

'No. I didn't dabble, apart from the occasional joint. I was more into beer at that age.'

Whitney doubted there was anything else he could help them with, but at least they were getting a better idea of what had been happening at the time the girls went missing.

'We may wish to speak to you again, so don't leave the city without contacting me first.' Whitney handed him her card.

'Am I a suspect?'

'We're in the early stages of the investigation and you are central to our enquiries.'

'But I didn't do anything.'

'In which case you have nothing to worry about.'

Whitney opened the door to the examination room and they left. Once outside she turned to George.

'Well?'

'His mannerisms didn't indicate guilt. He was ashamed and panicked that his past had come back to haunt him, but I do believe him.'

'I agree. Let's get back to the station and push forward with finding this second dealer.'

The drive back was relatively quick and they headed back to the incident room.

Whitney called everyone to attention and waited until all eyes were focused on her.

'We've just returned from visiting Nigel Young, the optometrist, who sold drugs for Shaw after the girls left him and began selling for another dealer. Something that Shaw had neglected to tell us. Young also mentioned that Shaw had argued with the girls and, afterwards, made threats against them, but we don't know if he followed them through. Ellie, please arrange for George and me to visit the prison again first thing tomorrow morning, so we can find out who this second dealer is.' She turned to George. 'Is that okay with you?'

'Yes, that's fine.'

'Brian, have you been to see Shaw's wife yet?'

'Yes, guv. We arrived back a few minutes before you. She'd been at the hospital this morning when we called. We only chatted to her for a short time. She wasn't well.'

'What did she tell you?'

'She confirmed that Shaw was involved in drug dealing in the 80s but said she knew nothing of the two girls, as she didn't get involved in the *business*. She was on drugs herself at that time and couldn't really remember much. I asked her about Nigel Young and she said the name rang a bell but that was all. She couldn't tell us anything about his relationship with Shaw. It was a wasted journey.'

'I disagree.' Whitney said. 'Every little piece of information adds to the picture. Our main priority now is to discover who this other dealer was and interview him. Brian, contact Kathleen Henderson, and ask her if she thought Shaw and the girls were arguing when she saw them.'

'Yes, guv.'

'Shaw has got a lot to answer for when we see him tomorrow, and I won't accept him fobbing us off.'

Chapter 16

I turn on the television, weary after spending several hours in the garden digging over the empty borders so the soil could be prepared for next year's planting. I know it will be worth it, when everything is in full bloom, but every part of me aches and all I want to do is settle down with a cup of coffee and a biscuit. Old age is no joke.

I drop on to the sofa and, no sooner do I relax into it when my body tenses as I stare open-mouthed at the TV.

Images of Oak Tree Farm fill the screen. The whole area is cordoned off, and a lone yellow digger is stationed to one side.

Dear God. This can't be happening.

I lean forward to ensure I don't miss a word that the newsreader is saying.

They've found the bodies. After all this time.

How?

They've been there for years and now suddenly they've been dug up? I watch further as the cameras pan the scene. It's unrecognisable from how I remember it.

I knew there were plans for a housing development on the farm but hadn't realised it was going to be on the exact spot where the bodies had been left. I should have checked, and then done something about it. But the thought didn't even cross my mind.

Thousands of acres to choose from and the development ended up there.

What were the odds?

I don't know what to do. Are the police going to be knocking on my door anytime soon?

That's stupid. There's no way they can link me to it. I need to stop panicking.

I'll have to weather this storm like I had to when it all happened.

I've thought about the girls over the years but have trained myself to put them to the back of my mind. I'm mostly successful, but every now and again, the thoughts rear their ugly heads and capture me in their grasp.

Then I tell myself that I can't change anything. It's something that has to be lived with. Forever.

Will there be any DNA on the bodies after all this time? I've no idea how the science works.

Even if there is, there shouldn't be any of mine though because I didn't touch them with my bare hands.

My eyes are glued to the screen as they interview the farmer and he explains how his digger operator came across the bones during the excavation.

I can't believe they managed to identify the bodies so quickly. There was nothing personal left on them which could be used and even if there was, you'd think that after this length of time it would have all degraded.

Technology these days is frightening. Thank goodness it wasn't around when they died.

Will they be able to identify how they actually died?

It was an accident. A fatal accident. I hadn't intended it to happen.

They weren't nice girls, though. I shouldn't be saying that, under *the circumstances, but it's the truth. It was their own fault that they ended up there. No one else can be blamed.*

I'm not excusing what happened.

Their families didn't deserve to lose them in that way.

But it was out of my hands and I'll do whatever it takes to make sure I'm not caught.

Chapter 17

'Do you know what time you'll be back?' Ross asked her, while they were eating breakfast on Saturday morning.

George had forgotten that she'd arranged to spend the day with him, when she'd agreed to go back to the prison with Whitney, and he'd already booked for them to see a performance of *Hamlet* late afternoon, at a theatre in Oxford, close to where he lived.

'We should be back by lunchtime. I'm sorry to change our plans.'

'I've got plenty of work to be getting on with this morning. I'll go home and you can drive out to my place later?'

'Yes, that would be perfect.' She finished her coffee, rinsed and placed her mug in the dishwasher. As she passed Ross, she leant down and gave him a kiss goodbye. 'I'll leave you to lock up.' She'd given him his own key several weeks ago. Whitney had thought that was *big*. She'd done it for convenience, not for any other more significant reason.

She drove to the station to collect Whitney. Thankfully,

her pass had come through which meant she could go upstairs without having to wait to be escorted. When she entered the incident room, it was a hive of activity, even though it was the weekend. Brian, Doug and Meena were sitting at their desks, although there was no sign of Frank. Whitney was in her office and as George got closer, she saw the phone held to the officer's ear. Whitney glanced up and beckoned her in.

'Okay?' Whitney asked as she ended the call.

'Fine, thanks,' George said.

'Do you fancy going out for lunch later, after we've seen Shaw? A little bit of downtime would do us good.'

'I can't. Ross and I had arranged to spend the day together. I'm going over there once we've finished.'

'Crap. Was he annoyed with you disappearing for the morning?'

'No, he wasn't. He understands that working with you is important. He's working on a commission of a dog for one of his regular customers, so he now has more time to spend on it. When it comes to his work, he's a perfectionist.'

That was one of the reasons why they were a good fit. She liked things to be perfect, too.

'Any talk of moving in together?'

'Why do you keep asking? We're taking it one day at a time. It works well for me.'

'Okay, I won't mention it again,' Whitney said, holding up both hands. 'Let's go, the traffic shouldn't be too heavy on a Saturday.'

'I noticed everyone was in except Frank. Why's that?' she asked, as they left Whitney's office and were heading down the corridor to the lift.

'I don't need them all in and you know how Frank likes his weekends off. Not to mention we don't want to blow the overtime budget on a cold case. The super wouldn't be too happy about that.'

'That makes sense.'

When they arrived at the prison, Shaw was waiting for them in the same room as the previous day.

'What are you offering me?' he asked the moment they walked in to interview him.

'Nothing,' Whitney said, pulling out a chair and sitting down.

George did the same and then glanced across at Shaw. He clearly had no idea what they knew, judging by his complacent attitude.

'We've been to see Nigel Young, and he is fairly certain that he was with you during the afternoon of the 7th of May, after you'd been with Jayne and Anita.'

'See. I told you.' He sucked in a small breath.

So, he had been worried about it.

'But … we don't know what you did after you left him, and that's what we're interested in knowing because according to Young, you were very angry with the girls.'

'Nah. That's rubbish.' His eyes darted from Whitney to George and back again.

Was he bluffing? Did he know?

'They'd started working for another dealer, which you were extremely unhappy about.'

'I don't remember.' He shrugged.

'You'd better start remembering because we under-stand that you spent much of the afternoon talking about what you were going to do to get back at them for leaving you and going to the new dealer.'

His arms were on the table and his fists clenched into tight balls. 'Okay. I was mad because after I showed them what to do, and told them who all my customers were, they pissed off to work for someone else. I didn't mean the threats. I was just sounding off.'

'What were you going to do about it?'

'Nothing to the girls. Cross my heart.' He made a sign on his chest. 'I just got Nigel to work for me instead. Boys were buying more drugs than girls at that time so I thought he could get me more customers.'

He looked directly at them and his blink rate was normal. He was telling the truth.

'I want to know about this other drug dealer.'

'His name was Cyril.'

'Cyril what?'

'I dunno.' He shrugged.

'I'm going to need more than that. What else can you tell me?'

'He lived on the Flaxton estate and everyone called him Hopper because he limped. He was short and had brown hair.'

'Tattoos? Other distinguishing features?'

'I don't know.'

'Were the girls working for him when you spoke to them last?'

'Yeah. I got told by a mate the morning of the day I went to speak to them at the school. I told 'em they'd be sorry if they nicked any of my customers.'

'Why didn't you tell us this yesterday?'

'I knew you'd never believe me. You'd think I killed 'em, and I didn't.'

'Did they give a reason why they'd gone to work for him?'

'Money. He paid them more.'

'Did you offer to increase their money to stop them from leaving?'

'No, because I'd got Nigel. I was going to drop them,

anyway. Girls like that couldn't be trusted. They giggled all the time and were a pain in the arse.'

'That's not the way to talk about murder victims,' Whitney said.

'I still didn't do it and don't know anything about it. I saw them that day at lunchtime, and afterwards was with Nigel for the whole afternoon. Then I went home. You can ask my wife.'

'She has already been interviewed.'

His eyes flashed. 'Leave her out of it. She's not well.'

'You've just suggested we ask her. We pre-empted that.'

'What did she tell you?' he asked, panic in his voice.

Had he been intending to tell her what to say?

'She spoke to my officers but wasn't much help because, according to her, she was out of it a lot of the time during the 80s.'

'Did she say I wasn't at home with her?'

'No, because she couldn't remember.'

'You have to believe me. I had nothing to do with their deaths. This could ruin everything.' He grimaced.

'We'll be speaking to the other dealer, if we can find him,' Whitney said, ignoring his comment. 'We may be back.'

'What about you helping me get parole?' Shaw asked.

'I don't think that's a priority at the moment.'

Whitney stood, and George followed. They walked in silence until out of the prison and made their way to the car.

'I'll call Ellie with Cyril's name and description so she can crack on with finding him,' Whitney said, once they were seated. 'You can drop me off at the station and then go see Ross. Are you doing anything special?'

'We're going out for lunch and then to see *Hamlet* in Oxford. Ross has been looking forward to it.'

'Aren't you?'

'It's not my favourite Shakespeare play, but I'm sure it will be just fine.'

'Look at you being all compromising,' Whitney said, grinning.

'I'm not even going to bother to answer that,' she said.

'Only because you know I'm right.'

'How are you getting on?' Whitney asked Ellie, once she'd arrived back.

'I might have a hit. I've been looking through police records and other databases. His name is Cyril West, and he's got a record as long as your arm for drug offences and other petty crimes. He's seventy-eight. But there is something else, guv.' Ellie bit down on her bottom lip.

What was she nervous about telling her?

'What is it?' she asked.

Whitney scanned the office and all eyes were in their direction. Did they know what Ellie was about to say?

'He's living in Cumberland Court,' Ellie said.

Whitney's heart sank. Crap.

'Isn't that the place where your mum lives, guv?' Doug said.

'Yes, that's the one. I don't recognise his name, not that I know many of the residents. How long has he been living there?'

'About six months.'

'Show me his photo?'

She leant in to look at the screen on the officer's desk.

'Here,' Ellie said, pulling it up.

She scrutinised the picture. 'I haven't seen him, but he might have seen me, though.'

She hoped not, in case there were any repercussions against her mum.

'I'll go with you,' Brian said. 'Shall we go now?'

'No, we'll go tomorrow. That way I have plenty of time to make the necessary arrangements for him to be taken somewhere out of the way to interview, probably his bedroom.'

'I can't make it tomorrow,' Brian said.

'Why not?' she asked.

'I've got something on,' he said, his voice cagey. 'It's personal. Surely, we should see him immediately if he's pivotal to the case. He could be our murderer.'

What was this mysterious personal thing? He knew they were working over the weekend. If he'd wanted time off, he should have asked. Like Frank had.

'No. This is a very old cold case and I want to keep it low-key. There's nothing to be gained by rushing in to see West, all guns blazing. We'll get more out of him if we do the interview in a relaxed, informal way. I also need to be mindful of the fact that he may know my mum. It's not a problem, Brian. I'll take George with me instead. Her expertise with his body language will be of great assistance. Does he have any family, Ellie?'

'A daughter, but she's in Somerset and doesn't live close by.'

'Good. The chances of her being there are minimal, if that. It means he's not going anywhere, and at this point has no idea that we're looking for him. With Shaw being in prison, and Nigel Young having no desire to get involved, especially as he didn't even know the identity of West, I think we're quite safe to wait until tomorrow. I'll speak to the super and let her know our plans. Her car's in the car park so I know she's here today. Then I'll contact the home and make the arrangements to visit.'

Chapter 18

Whitney knocked on the door of Clyde's office.

'Come in.'

Whitney entered and the super looked up from her desk and smiled. Such a different response from when she used to see Jamieson. She really needed to stop comparing the two. He'd gone, and this was a brand-new relationship. Not to mention, George would have a field day analysing her if she continued.

'Morning, ma'am.'

'Sit,' Clyde said, gesturing to one of the chairs in front of her desk. 'I want to know how the investigation is going.'

'We're making good progress and have identified the man who the girls were last seen speaking to. His name is Reginald Shaw, and he's a drug dealer who's now in prison, as you are aware. We've also learnt that after speaking to Jayne and Anita he spent the afternoon with a Nigel Young, who was a student at the school at the time. He's now an optometrist working in the city.'

'Optometrist?'

'Yes. It seemed he pulled himself together. It transpired that the girls had been selling drugs for Shaw and they left to go to work for another dealer, Cyril West. Young started selling for Shaw in their place. He told us that Shaw was angry about the girls leaving and he'd made threats against them.'

'Do you think Shaw is responsible for their deaths?'

'We're not sure and he denies it, obviously. DS Chapman has been to see his wife, but she's ill and doesn't recall much from those days. We've also identified this second dealer who's in a care home in Lenchester. I'm going to see him tomorrow morning with Dr Cavendish.'

Should she mention her mum was there? No. There wasn't a need to.

'Excellent. I'm pleased that the case is moving forward. We should—'

A knock at the door interrupted her. It opened before the super could speak, and Whitney turned around to see Dickhead Douglas standing there.

Her stomach dropped.

'Morning, Helen. I've just come in to see …' He trailed off as he stared at Whitney, the warmth leaving his eyes, his expression going from amiable to one of contempt. 'I didn't know you were in here,' he said to Whitney.

'Yes, sir. I was discussing my case with the super.'

'Is there anything I can help you with, sir?' Clyde said.

'It will wait. I don't wish to talk with other people present.' He turned and headed out of the office.

There was silence for several seconds.

'Sorry about that,' Clyde said.

'It's fine,' Whitney said shrugging.

'It's not,' Clyde said in a cold tone.

'It's how he always is when we see each other.' Whitney

tried to make light of it. If she didn't it would drive her crazy and she wasn't going to let that happen.

'As I've already said, you can rest assured I won't let him interfere in your career.'

'Thank you, ma'am.'

'Before you go, I wanted to ask you something.'

'Yes, ma'am?'

'You mentioned during the interview that you were happy staying as a DCI and I've been giving it some thought. Is there any reason for this?'

'Both my mother and brother are in local care homes. In fact, my mum is in the one we're going to visit tomorrow as she has dementia and needs twenty-four-hour care. My father died many years ago so he isn't around to help. My brother has irreparable brain damage following an attack on him when he was young by a group of teenagers. He was beaten up badly, and it left him like that.'

And that was her life in a nutshell. Something caught in her throat and she swallowed it down.

'I'm sorry to hear that, Whitney. It explains why you have stayed at this force for so long, despite who else was here.'

Whitney nodded, assuming she meant Douglas.

'I'm committed to my work, but I do have them to consider. I also have a daughter, Tiffany, who's in Australia.'

She hadn't intended blurting out her whole life history, but it had just happened.

'How old is she?'

'Twenty-one. She was at university but decided to take a year out. I'm hoping when she returns, she'll go back. What about you, ma'am? How are you settling in here at Lenchester?'

'It's all going very well, thank you. We have a lovely building here.'

That was debatable.

'Have your family settled?'

Was that a step too far? She didn't want to intrude, but she was interested.

'Yes, thank you. I've two teenage boys who are virtually self-sufficient, and they're away at boarding school, so it made it much easier for me to move over to Lenchester.'

Boarding school. Had Clyde gone there, too? Would she get on well with George?

'I'd better be going, ma'am. I need to organise the visit to interview West.'

'You mentioned that it's the same home your mother is in. Do you see that being an issue?'

'No, ma'am.'

'If you're happy with that, then I'll trust your judgement. Do remember, if there are any issues, or there's anything you'd like to discuss, come to me and we can speak in confidence. I'm happy to have you in this position. We're going to make an excellent team.'

'Thank you, ma'am. I appreciate you saying that.'

She left the room and sauntered down the corridor, smiling. She thought back to her meetings with Jamieson when each time she'd left his office she was tense and wound up. Being with Clyde was a walk in the park.

If it wasn't for Dickhead, work would be good. But the new super would have her back. She was confident about that.

Chapter 19

'You're looking apprehensive,' George said to Whitney as they sat in the car outside Cumberland Court, the large Edwardian care home where both her mother and Cyril West lived. There were only twenty long-term residents there but as she'd never come across West during her visits, and her mum hadn't mentioned him, Whitney hoped that they didn't have anything to do with each other.

She'd timed their visit for late Sunday morning so that the staff would have done all of the usual morning tasks of handing out medication, getting residents up, and giving them breakfast. Lorraine, the manager, had agreed to ensure that West was taken to his room. It meant they could go straight there and reduce the risk of bumping into her mum and having to explain what they were doing there.

She was hoping to have a quick chat with her mum after the interview as she hadn't seen her for over a week, because of the new team and the case.

'That's because I'm hoping West won't recognise me, in case he takes it out on Mum. I explained to the manager that we're here on police business and asked her to arrange for West to be taken to his room to wait for us.'

'What's she going to tell him?' George asked.

'I've said not to mention who we are but to keep it vague and say somebody wants to come and visit him. Hopefully he won't ask too many questions. Although I'm sure she'll be able to field them. We'll sign in first and then we'll go straight to his room which I believe is on the first floor.'

'How close to your mother's room is he?'

'I'm not sure, but to be on the safe side I've suggested that they put her in the day room to watch the television. It's where she usually is at this time of day so it shouldn't cause any problems. I don't want her to know we're here in case I don't have time to go and see her after West's interview as it might confuse her.'

'If you're worried, why didn't you let Brian do the interview instead of you?'

'He wasn't at the prison when we visited Shaw, so he'd be seeing West without the information we have. As it happens, I did ask him to come with me today, but he had something personal on. It annoyed me, as he hadn't mentioned wanting the day off in advance.'

'It must have been important if he couldn't come with you, as he doesn't want to get in your bad books.'

'I have no idea,' she said, waving her hands. 'He didn't say, and I didn't ask. What with that and the Dickhead incident, yesterday wasn't a great day.'

'What incident?'

She had intended to tell George after it all happened, and then remembered her outing with Ross, so had decided not to bother her.

'I was in with Clyde, and he walked in wanting to speak to her. He didn't notice me straight away, but you should have seen the look of disdain on his face when he did. He left the room soon after.'

'What did the superintendent say?'

'She reminded me that she had my back. Not in those words but that's what she meant. It remains to be seen whether she has, or whether Douglas will get the better of her. Come on, let's go in. I can't interview with thoughts of Douglas in my head.'

Whitney drew in a breath, before she opened the door and stepped out of the car. Once inside the building, she signed them both in and they took the stairs to the first floor and headed down the corridor. When they reached West's room Whitney tapped gently on the door and opened it.

'Mr West,' she said.

'Yes.'

The elderly man was seated in his wheelchair beside the window, his head slightly bent over. He was bald, apart from a few strands of grey hair around the back of his head, and his skin was sallow. He didn't look well.

'I'm Detective Chief Inspector Walker and this is Dr Cavendish.'

'What's this about? They wouldn't tell me.' He stared directly at Whitney, his eyes alert, and at odds with his frail body. 'I've seen you in here before.'

Damn. Exactly what she didn't want to hear.

'Yes, I'm here sometimes.'

'You visit the woman with dementia who sits in the TV room.'

'That's correct,' Whitney said. 'But that's not why we're here to see you. We want to ask you about two girls whose bodies have recently been found. They were murdered in 1980. You might know about it as it's been on the news recently.'

'I don't watch the news or read the paper,' he said.

She scrutinised him for any deception or lack of understanding, but he seemed perfectly lucid and the muscles around his mouth were relaxed. Was he lying? George would know.

'How long have you been here?' she asked.

'A few months. I had an accident and social services said I couldn't take care of myself. They made me come here as there was no one to look after me.'

She certainly understood that, as she'd been in the exact situation with her mum and brother.

'Do you keep in touch with your daughter?' she asked, remembering that Ellie had mentioned her.

'I ain't seen Sissy in years. I don't even know where she is. It's just me on my own.'

Whitney knew that Sissy was in Somerset, but it wasn't for her to tell him. The daughter would have to make contact herself if she wanted to.

'What accident did you have?' George asked.

'Fell down the front steps and bust my leg and arm.'

'Are you sure you have no idea about the two bodies that were found?' Whitney asked.

'I've already told you, so stop trying to trip me up.' He glared at Whitney.

'The dead girls were Anita Bailey and Jayne Kennedy.' His eyes flickered. 'You remember them?'

'Yes.' He nodded.

Now they were getting somewhere.

'We understand they started working for you, selling drugs to school kids,' Whitney said.

'Yeah. So what?' he replied, his voice as calm as if they'd been discussing the weather.

'And you think that's okay, do you?' Whitney snapped, unable to hide her disgust at his behaviour.

She shouldn't have spoken like that, but his attitude was winding her up. No doubt George would have something to say about her confrontational manner.

'You're talking years ago.' He shrugged. 'I don't even think about it.'

'According to our sources, Anita and Jayne went missing shortly after they started working for you. Didn't you think that was strange?' Whitney asked.

'The papers said they'd run away.'

'Did you believe it?' Whitney asked.

'Why wouldn't I?'

'Weren't you surprised that they just disappeared without telling you?'

'A bit, but I had other sellers to do their work. It wasn't like it was a full-time job, or anything.'

Whitney tensed. She could shake the man for his cavalier attitude.

'When did you last see the girls?' Whitney asked.

He stared at her, as if she'd asked a ridiculous question. 'You've got to be kidding me. It was years ago. I can't even remember what I have for breakfast every day.'

'Think about it,' Whitney pushed.

'It wasn't the day they went missing,' he said.

'How can you be sure, if you don't remember exactly?'

'Because it was in the papers and there were posters everywhere saying the last time they'd been seen, and it made me think that I didn't see them that day.'

'The parents didn't believe the girls had run away and that's why they put up the posters. What did you think? Did you agree?'

'No idea.' He shrugged. 'What else do you want to know? And make it quick. I need the toilet, and unless you're going to take me, you'd better call a carer to help.'

Was he telling the truth, or did he just want to get rid of them?

'The last person who was seen talking to them, other than students and teachers, was Reginald Shaw.'

He turned his nose up. 'Oh, him.'

'Yes, and he was the person who told us they'd started working for you.'

'That sounds like the bastard. Next you'll be telling me he said I killed them. Did he?'

'No.'

'Did he tell you *why* they started working for me?'

'You paid them more money?'

'He's a liar.' He leant forward slightly in his chair and gave a raspy cough.

'What was the *truth*?' Whitney said. 'You tell me.'

'His stuff was crap and one of the boys at the school died after taking some.'

Whitney and George exchanged a glance. This was new. Was it relevant?

'Are you sure? This is the first we've heard of it.'

'That's what the girls told me, and they should know because they were the ones who sold it to the dead kid.'

'Do you know the name of the student who died?'

'No.'

She'd get Ellie on to it.

'How long did the girls work for you?' Whitney asked.

'A couple a weeks, at most, before they ran away. Or whatever happened to them. At the start they were working for me and Shaw at the same time.'

'Did you try to find them after they'd disappeared?'

'No. Why would I? There was never a shortage of kids who wanted to make some easy money. I got someone else to do their round.'

'Is there anything else you can tell us? Do you have an alibi for the day the girls went missing?'

'If I do, I can't remember. All I know is I didn't see the girls on the day they went missing. I've already told you that.'

'If you do think of anything else, let me know,' Whitney said, handing him a card. 'I'll ask a carer to come up to take you to the toilet.'

'Don't bother. I've got a bag.' He laughed as he pulled up his trouser leg to reveal a catheter. 'Sucker,' he muttered under his breath, but loud enough for Whitney to hear.

They left his room and once out of earshot Whitney turned to George.

'We need the name of the student who died. If Anita and Jayne sold him the drugs that killed, that would give someone a strong motive to get revenge.'

'Agreed. Are you going to see your mother, now?'

'Yes, if you don't mind,' Whitney said, as she checked her watch.

'I'll wait for you in the car.'

'Thanks. I won't be long as it's almost time for her lunch, then you can drop me back to the station.'

They headed downstairs and parted as Whitney wandered towards the day room. She walked inside and looked across to where her mum usually sat. The chair was empty. She glanced around to see if she was sitting somewhere else, but she wasn't. She turned and marched back to the reception desk where Angela, one of the care assistants, was seated.

'If you're looking for your mum, she wasn't feeling well so Riki's taken her to her room for a rest.'

Whitney tensed. 'What's the matter?'

'She had a headache from not sleeping very well last night. Nothing to worry about.'

'I'll go to see her.'

She headed over to the stairs and jogged up them. When she reached her mum's room the door was open slightly and she popped her head around. Riki was standing by the bed and smiled when she saw Whitney.

'Come in,' the care assistant said. 'She's just fallen asleep.'

'I was hoping to speak to her,' Whitney said, unable to hide the despondency in her voice.

'She's not having a good day, today. She kept asking me who I was and whether I knew where Roger was because they were meant to be going out for lunch at The Swan pub.'

'That's my dad. He's been dead for twelve years. The Swan was their favourite place to eat out, and where they went to celebrate birthdays and anniversaries.' She sighed loudly and shook her head.

In a way, she was glad her mum was asleep because when she was in her own little world and didn't know Whitney, or remember anything about their life, it just about crucified her. And it was going to get worse. Whitney had been warned there would come a time when her mum wouldn't know her at all. She couldn't bear the thought of that happening. How would Rob cope? He sort of understood their mum wasn't well but didn't grasp the full extent of it. How could he?

She'd have to make the most of when her mum was lucid and in touch with reality. But for how long?

Chapter 20

When Whitney arrived for work in the morning she was surprised to see Ellie already seated at her desk working. She hung her coat and scarf on the back of the door and wandered through into the incident room and over to see the officer.

'You're in early.'

Ellie glanced up and smiled. 'I stayed overnight at my boyfriend's house and he had an early start this morning, so I left when he did. I've got a lot to do and it's always easier when the office is empty.'

Whitney stared open-mouthed at the officer. Ellie was as bad as Matt, her old sergeant, for keeping her personal life close to her chest. This was the first time she'd ever volunteered any information about her boyfriend, who Whitney knew nothing about. She'd love to find out more but knew to wait until Ellie was ready to tell her.

'Yes, the noise can get distracting at times. How's it going? Have you found our dead student yet?' She was anxious to move the investigation forward, now they actually had more to work with.

'I was just making some final checks, but yes. I think so. I've looked through all the coroner's reports for the six months leading up to the time the two girls went missing and discovered a Justin Robertson, who was found dead in his bed by his parents the day after his sixteenth birthday. His death was recorded as accidental, following an adverse reaction to taking an amphetamine drug.'

'Sixteen.' Whitney shook her head, letting out a sigh. 'What a waste of a life. Have you been able to track down his family?'

'His parents, Peggy and Kenneth, still live in Lenchester. They're at 65 Hampton Street, which is close to St Paul's school.'

'Good work on finding everything so quickly. Can you tell me anything else about the family?'

'His parents have retired … they're both in their seventies. Mr Robertson was an electrician and Mrs Robertson worked for over thirty years for the council in their accounts department. Justin was their only child.'

'I couldn't think of anything worse,' Whitney muttered. 'How on earth were they able to deal with it?'

'I don't know, guv. It must have been a horrible time for them,' Ellie said, as she returned to staring at her screen.

Whitney headed for her office, pulled out her phone and called George.

'We've identified the young boy who died,' she said, once George had answered. 'Is there any chance you can come with me to speak to his parents?'

'Not today, sorry. I've got back-to-back meetings and I've no idea what time they'll finish. Late, knowing the staff here.'

Damn.

'No problem. I'll take Brian.'

'That's a much better option,' George said.

Was it? She was still miffed at him being unable to come with her yesterday, but she couldn't sideline him. Maybe he would tell her what was so important he wasn't able to work. She'd use their time together as an opportunity to get to know him better. George would be proud of her.

She grabbed her coat and returned to the office, noting that the rest of the team had arrived. She called them to attention.

'I'm shortly going to go and see the parents of Justin Robertson who died from taking drugs our victims sold him. Brian, I want you with me. They still live in Lenchester, so it won't take us long to get there.'

'Yes, guv.'

'Where are we on the other lines of enquiry?'

'I've identified the three farm workers,' Brian said. 'Alf Simpson, Bert Best and Wayne Cross. Simpson is dead, so we can't interview him. Cross is in Rugby and Best is here in Lenchester.'

'Good. You can go when we return from seeing the Robertsons. Take Meena with you.'

She hadn't yet witnessed any issues between them, despite what she'd learnt on their first day and hoped that the more they worked together the more their relationship would develop. She had no problems with Meena, who so far was conscientious and hard-working.

'Yes, guv.'

'Frank, Doug. Anything from the past pupils and teachers of St Paul's?'

'I've spoken to several teachers,' Doug said. 'And none of them had anything good to say about the girls, in particular Anita. They were disruptive, rude and universally disliked.'

'It was the same with the students,' Frank added. 'All I'm getting is confirmation of what we've already learnt from the interview with Kathleen Henderson. They weren't liked, and kids were scared of them.' He paused. 'You know, if you asked me who I went to school with, I'd be hard-pressed to remember one or two. But every person I spoke to remembered Anita and Jayne very well. That's saying something.'

'Did you learn anything new about the day they disappeared?'

'No, guv. Maybe the whole class got together and killed them. Like a joint murder,' Frank said.

'Don't even joke about it,' she said, not wanting to contemplate it.

'You've been reading too many Stephen King books, that's your trouble,' Doug said.

'Stephen who?' Frank frowned.

'Surely even you know who he is. Remember the film *Misery?*'

'Yes. It was great.'

'It was based on one of King's books.'

'Well, why didn't you say so in the first place?'

'I didn't think you'd—'

'Button it, you two,' Whitney said wagging her finger in their direction. 'Come on, Brian, let's go. We'll leave the children to it. We'll take your car.'

Brian strode over to the coat hook which stood in the corner of the room, took his navy jacket from the hanger and shrugged it on. He was certainly well dressed. Probably the best dressed out of the team. Was it a throwback to his Met days? They left the room and walked down the corridor to the lift. The door opened to reveal Douglas standing in the corner.

Crap. Part of her wanted to turn around and take the stairs, but Brian had already stepped into the lift. Douglas ignored Whitney and smiled at Brian.

'Good to see you, son.'

She blinked. *Son?* What the hell was going on here? How did Dickhead know Brian?

'Good to see you too, sir,' Brian said standing right next to him.

That suited her fine, as she stood on the opposite side of the lift, as close to the edge as she could get.

'How's it going in the new team?' Douglas asked, in his usual pompous voice.

'Very well, thank you, sir.' Brian glanced in her direction, but she didn't acknowledge him, instead kept staring ahead at the lift door.

'There's a match coming up at the weekend, will you be there?' Douglas asked.

'Yes, sir. I'm playing at right back. Will you make it?'

Seriously? They socialised as well?

'Most definitely. We've got to beat them if we want a chance of winning the league. We're relying on you.'

Were they discussing football? Surely Dickhead wasn't playing, not at his age. Unless he was in goal as he wouldn't have to do much moving about in that position. Just a bit of lolloping around. She allowed herself a tiny smile.

'We will,' Brian said, emphatically. 'All the lads are determined to make it happen.'

Remind her to bring out her cheerleading outfit. She could go and wave her pom-poms. Preferably in Dickhead's face.

'Glad to hear it. Where are you off to now?' Douglas asked.

'Interviewing the parents of a dead student.'

'Which case are you working on?'

Brian glanced at her and she gave a nod. She couldn't have stopped him from telling Douglas, who had every right to know, but it pleased her that Brian sought her permission first.

'The two teenage girls found on Oak Tree Farm who'd been buried there since 1980.'

'Oh, yes, of course. Superintendent Clyde told me about that.' The lift stopped at the ground floor and they all got out. 'Well, keep up the good work,' he said to Brian, totally blanking Whitney.

They headed in the opposite direction and she was quiet until they were out of earshot of Douglas.

'I didn't know you and the chief super socialised,' she said to Brian, forcing her voice to stay calm.

'I knew him from the Met, before he moved to the Regional Force. He's a good bloke. Gets things done.'

A good bloke. Not if you wear a skirt.

'Did you know he was moving to Lenchester?' she asked, forcing her expression to remain neutral.

'No, guv. But I was pleased when I found out. Didn't he used to work here, years ago?'

'Yes. He was a sergeant when I joined the force.'

'Did you know each other?'

'Yes, why?'

'Because neither of you acknowledged one another.'

'It's a long story,' she said waving her hand dismissively. And not one she was prepared to share.

'He's helping coach the Lenchester police football team.'

'You've joined it already?' Was that why he couldn't make it yesterday, because he was socialising?

'It's a joint Willsden and Lenchester team. We've got some ace players and with the chief super involved we'll kick arse.'

'Oh.' It was all she would allow herself to say, not trusting that she could keep her true feelings hidden. George would be proud of her restraint. 'Let's get going. The journey to the Robertsons' house will take us about fifteen minutes.'

Chapter 21

Mr and Mrs Robertson lived in a 1930s semi-detached house in a working-class area of the city. It was similar to the area in which Whitney had been brought up and was mostly respectable. The dodgy parts she remembered well as when she worked in uniform she'd spent many a shift there sorting out disturbances, some of which turned very nasty.

Before getting out of the car, she looked at Brian. 'Remember the rules this time. I'll do the talking and you listen.'

She couldn't make it any plainer, so he had no excuse for not following.

'What if I think of something that you haven't asked?' Brian said.

'Chances are, I have thought about it and dismissed it as unnecessary at this point, so unless you're a mind reader, I talk, you observe.'

She injected a sharp tone to her voice. Their relationship wouldn't work if he tried to second-guess her all of the time. She understood that he wanted to impress her, as the senior officer, but he also needed to learn when and where it was appropriate.

'Okay, guv. I get it.'

'Remember, we don't know what state these parents are going to be in when we ask them about Justin. It might have been many years since he died, but I'm sure that day is etched indelibly on their minds and for us to dredge it up will most likely be extremely difficult for them. They won't ever forget losing their child, especially in those circumstances.'

'Yes, guv, I do realise it's not going to be easy for them. I'm not totally insensitive, you know.'

Did he just roll his eyes? She didn't think she'd come across as preachy but …

'Come on, let's go.'

They walked down the short path and past the well-kept garden which had a small square of lawn with neat borders and was filled with green shrubs around the edge.

The rust coloured door had a gold knocker in the middle and Whitney used it to tap. After a few moments, she could hear shuffling footsteps and an elderly man answered. He was about five feet ten and wiry. The red and black checked shirt he was wearing hung off his shoulders.

'Yes?' he said, his pale, alert grey eyes staring back at them.

'Mr Robertson?' Whitney asked.

'That's me. Who are you?'

'I'm Detective Chief Inspector Walker and this is Detective Sergeant Chapman.' She held out her warrant card and he peered intently at it. 'We'd like to come in and have a word with you, if we may.'

'What's it about?'

'We'd rather not talk on the street.'

'If you don't tell me then you can't come in,' he said, folding his arms. His veined hands were pale and covered with brown age spots.

She was surprised by his tone as she'd shown him her identification and they weren't attempting to enter his house for unscrupulous reasons. Had he been the victim of a crime in the past involving people coming into his house?

'It's about Justin.'

At the mention of his son's name, Mr Robertson's face lost its colour, but he quickly pulled himself together.

'I'm sorry if I came across as rude, but we hear all these stories about people trying to get into your homes by pretending to be workmen or government officials and then they steal your possessions without you even realising. You can't be too careful.'

'I did show you my warrant card,' she said gently.

'They can fake those easily enough,' he said.

'I understand. It's better to be wary rather than too trusting when there are strangers around. May we come in now?'

'Yes, of course.' He opened the door fully so they could enter. 'My wife's in the sitting room. We were just about to have our morning coffee.'

She could murder a coffee. Coming face to face with Douglas had put her on edge. For now, though, it was more important they spoke to the couple about their son.

'We won't keep you long,' she said.

They followed him into a square room, which reminded her of the house she had lived in growing up. The walls were covered with woodchip paper which was painted a pale peach colour, and the carpet was a chocolate brown. Seated on a floral easy chair, that matched the three-seater sofa, was an elderly woman.

'It's the police, Peggy,' Mr Robertson said.

'What's happened?' she asked, her eyes wide, as she stood and stepped towards her husband, standing close to him.

She was about Whitney's height, round with short silver-grey hair that looked as if it had recently been set.

'We'd like to talk to you about Justin,' Whitney said.

The woman exchanged a glance with her husband, a worried expression on her face. 'What about him?'

'Please will you both sit down.' Whitney waited until they were seated on the sofa and then sat on the chair vacated by Mrs Robertson. Brian stood by the door. Was he doing that because of their last interview? She'd explain that in future he should sit as standing could be intimidating, especially with older people like the Robertsons. 'I know it must be hard to talk about Justin even after all this time.'

'Yes, it is' Mrs Robertson said, her eyes glistening.

'We're investigating the deaths of two girls who were in Justin's year at school.'

'The ones they found at the farm?' Mr Robertson asked.

'Yes, that's correct. The girls were Anita Bailey and Jayne Kennedy. Did you know them?'

'I'm not sure,' Mrs Robertson said. 'We might have seen them, but Justin had lots of friends and they would all come here after school. He said they liked it here because I did lots of baking. They'd go to his bedroom and play records. I still remember. It …'

'Why are you asking?' Mr Robertson said.

She sucked in a breath, bracing herself for delivering the news. 'We have been informed, although it's not confirmed, that they were the young women who sold Justin the amphetamine that resulted in his death.'

The silence enveloped them as the elderly couple took in the news. The only sign of movement was when Mrs Robertson took hold of her husband's hand and squeezed.

'We didn't know that,' Mr Robertson said. 'But surely you don't think we had something to do with the girls' deaths?' His voice tremored.

'Please don't worry, Mr Robertson. We're not here to accuse you. Our investigation has widened since discovering the girls were dealing at school and that Justin had died after taking a drug they'd possibly sold him. We want to get a fuller picture of the girls' lives and believe that speaking to you about Justin will help. I know this will be hard for you, but can you tell me about the time he died?'

Mrs Robertson drew in a breath and closed her eyes for a few seconds. 'It was a Friday night and Justin had gone out to a club in the city called The County with his friends to celebrate his sixteenth birthday. I'd dropped him off outside at eight, where he'd arranged to meet them.' She fiddled with the edge of the beige knitted cardigan she was wearing. 'I know none of them were eighteen, but we thought he'd be safe as so many kids from his school went there especially on a Friday. The management turned a blind eye to their ages. We thought it was better than having him roaming the streets. When he was there, he took some speed. It … it …' A single tear rolled down her cheek and she brushed it away. 'It affected him badly and he died in his sleep after he came home.' She paused for a few seconds. 'I-I knocked on his bedroom door late Saturday morning to tell him I was going shopping. When he didn't answer I went in and found him sprawled out on top of his covers, still dressed. His body was stone cold. He'd been dead for hours …' Her voice faded away.

A breath caught in Whitney's throat. The grief, even after all this time, was so raw.

'The coroner said Justin died from a heart attack and recorded his death as accidental,' Mr Robertson added.

'Did *anyone* ask you where Justin got the drug from?' Brian asked.

'No.' Mr Robertson shook his head.

'Do *you* know where he got it from?' Brian continued.

Whitney inwardly fumed. The answer to that was obvious, from what Mr Robertson had said a few moments ago. If Brian was going to interrupt, which she had specifically warned against, then he could at least have listened to the rest of the interview.

'No. It wasn't something we even considered, we were too upset at losing Justin,' Mr Robertson said. 'It really didn't matter where he bought it. Knowing wasn't going to change the fact that he'd been taken from us.'

'Do you have a photo of Justin we can look at?' Whitney asked, putting an end to the line of questioning as it was serving no purpose.

'Yes, I can show you his room as well, if you like. We haven't touched it since he died,' Mrs Robertson said.

Her body tensed. Had they kept his room intact for all these years? Tears welled in her eyes, but she blinked them away before anyone noticed.

'Yes, please,' she said.

She glanced at Brian. Was this affecting him, too? It didn't appear to be, there was no change in his expression.

Her heart went out to the elderly couple. Their whole life had come to a standstill because of what had happened, and it appeared it had never restarted.

They followed Mrs Robertson upstairs and when they reached the first door on the left she opened it and they walked in. The room smelt fresh and airy, and the curtains had been opened. A single bed stood along the back wall, and there were Manchester United football posters on every surface. It was as if Justin was alive and still slept in there.

She glanced at Mrs Robertson, whose pinched expression had changed and become more relaxed. Did spending time in her son's room have some sort of cathartic effect on her?

'Justin liked his football,' Whitney said, as she peered at the posters and the old-fashioned kit the players wore.

'Yes, he was a really good player. He had his heart set on becoming a professional, but I'm not sure he was good enough for that, though. Unfortunately, we never found out.' Her eyes glazed over.

'Sergeant Chapman plays football, too,' Whitney said.

She nodded at Brian, encouraging him to speak and make a connection with Mrs Robertson. They owed her that much, coming into their lives and wanting them to relive what had happened. 'Yes, I do,' he said, his voice flat as he continued looking around the room.

Clearly he hadn't got her message.

Whitney headed over to the chest of drawers, after seeing a photo in the centre. 'Who's the girl with Justin in this picture?'

'His girlfriend, Liz. They were serious and talking about getting engaged. I know they were young, and we really didn't want them to settle down so soon, but she was such a lovely girl. She kept in touch with us for a couple of years after Justin passed, while she was still at school. But after she went off to university, we didn't see her again.'

'Lenchester?' Whitney asked.

'No. She went down south but I don't remember where. We didn't blame her for wanting to start afresh and forget about what had happened. I think she felt responsible.'

'In what way?' Brian said, jumping in.

Now he decided to talk.

'They were out together celebrating Justin's birthday and she didn't stop him from taking the pills. It was the first time he'd tried it.' She paused. 'And the last …'

'Was taking the drug her idea?' Whitney asked.

'I don't think so, because she didn't take any.'

'Did Liz tell you where Justin got the drugs from?' Brian asked.

Whitney frowned. They'd already covered that earlier, did he think they were lying? Nothing she'd heard so far made her believe that was the case.

'No. My husband told you, when it was all happening, we didn't think to ask.'

'Do you mind if I take the photo with me?' Whitney said. 'I'll bring it back as soon as we've finished with it.'

'Yes, that's fine,' Mrs Robertson said. 'But please look after it.'

Whitney pulled out an evidence bag from her pocket and dropped the photo in its silver frame inside.

'I will. Can you tell me Liz's full name?'

'Elizabeth Franklin.'

'And you definitely don't remember meeting, or hearing anything about Anita and Jayne?' Whitney asked, as she scanned the room.

'No, I'm sorry. But that doesn't mean I didn't. It was so long ago, and he knew so many people …'

The woman was getting agitated and Whitney didn't want to make things any worse for them.

'It's no problem. Thank you very much for showing us around and talking to us about Justin, we really appreciate it.'

They followed her downstairs and then left. Once they returned to the car she turned to Brian.

'Let's get back to the station. I want Ellie to find the girlfriend. I hope she's fairly local as that would make things much easier for us.'

Chapter 22

Whitney was standing at the board, staring at the map when she spotted George walk in.

'Good morning,' George said when she reached her. 'Where are we off to?'

'Watford to see Elizabeth Franklin, who was Justin Robertson's girlfriend while they were at school. It shouldn't take long in your car and I'm sure you'll love to put your foot down on the motorway.'

'You echoed my thoughts. Is she expecting us?' she asked.

'No, I decided against warning her we were coming. She's an accountant and works for Glasson Ltd. We'll go there and hope she's at work. If she isn't, we will go to her house.'

'It's a long way to drive without an appointment,' she said.

'Then we'll go back another time. Just think of all those miles you can clock up,' Whitney said arching an eyebrow.

'I admit it would be a nice trip.'

'It shouldn't take us more than fifty minutes to get there,' Whitney said.

'Okay, I'm ready whenever you are.'

'Listen up, everyone. Dr Cavendish and I are going to see Elizabeth Franklin. We'll be back later. Before we go, Brian, feedback from your interviews with the farm workers.'

'Best is in his eighties and lives with his son. He kept repeating that farming was hard work and he worked on a farm for fifty years. He wasn't really with it so I couldn't push him. We got more out of Cross. According to him, the farm was well run during old Mr Gibson's time, but he thought Anthony was a waste of space.'

'Did he say why?'

'Yes. He said he was full of hot air, with lots of grand plans which came to nothing, because he didn't understand farming.'

'Damning, but not directly any help to the enquiry. Did you ask him about what the land was used for, especially where the burial site was?'

'Yes, guv. During his time the land was mainly arable. In the 70s and early 80s they mainly grew barley and gradually shifted to wheat. I showed him a photo of the burial site and he said that part of the farm was left unplanted because of it being close to the public right of way and kids and dogs were always running all over it.'

'Makes sense. Thanks, Brian.' She turned to George. 'Let's go.'

They headed out to the car and Whitney smiled at the thrilled expression on her friend's face as she started the engine and drove out into the traffic.

'What can you tell me about Elizabeth Franklin?' George asked.

'She's single and lives alone, according to Ellie. She

went out with Justin for two years and at sixteen their relationship was serious. They were even talking about getting engaged. Justin's parents approved of the couple being together and Elizabeth kept in touch with them until going off to university, two years after Justin died, and they didn't hear from her again after that. They believe Elizabeth felt guilty over what had happened, because she didn't stop him from taking the drug.'

'That often happens. You should address that in your questioning.'

'Yes, I will.'

'Is there something wrong, you don't seem your usual self?' George asked, glancing quickly at her.

'There is. I was going to tell you, but then decided not to bother you with it. It's about Brian. You're never going to believe this but he's friends with Douglas.'

'Close friends?'

'I've no idea but I do know that he's worked with Dickhead in the past and he thinks he's a *good bloke*. What the hell is that meant to mean? You've seen for yourself what an arsewipe he can be. And now I've got someone on my team who thinks he's a *good bloke*.'

'Brian could have said that because he didn't want to demean Douglas in front of you, as you're his superior officer,' George said.

'I'll reserve judgement on that.'

'How did you find this out?'

'We bumped into Dickhead in the lift and they started talking about football. Brian plays for the Lenchester police team and it seems that Dickhead is coaching them.'

'That doesn't make them friends.'

'No, but you should have heard the way Douglas was talking to him, as if they were best buddies.'

'Are you sure Douglas didn't do it on purpose to make

you think they were closer than they really are. As a chief superintendent it's not the sort of behaviour I'd condone or expect him to engage in, however, witnessing first-hand how he can be with you, I wouldn't discount it.'

'You're right, he could have done it just to wind me up. I wouldn't put it past him. But, having said that, I'll still have to be careful what I say to Brian in future, in case he tells Douglas.'

'But surely as chief superintendent he has a right to know everything that's going on in any case being investigated by all the teams at Lenchester.'

'On a macro level, of course he does. But he doesn't need to know all the details. It's … oh, never mind.' She gave a frustrated sigh.

'But that aside, are you finding working with Brian satisfactory?'

'If I forget about Dickhead, then he's not too bad. I just have to stop comparing him with Matt, which is hard because I liked Matt so much. I'm sure in time Brian will settle in.'

'What about your other new recruit, how's she doing?'

She shifted about in her seat, conscious that she'd hardly thought about Meena at all recently, as she'd been so busy focusing on Brian.

'I haven't had much to do with Meena so far, obviously, because this is our first case. I have no complaints, although I've not given her as much attention as she should have had.'

'I'm sure you'll be able to rectify that, and ensure she feels part of the team.'

The rest of the journey they chatted about less worrying things, which she was glad about as it meant she could relax more.

When they arrived at Glasson Ltd, George parked in

the car park and they headed through the double doors into the reception.

'I'm Detective Chief Inspector Walker and this is Dr Cavendish. We're from Lenchester CID.' Whitney held out her warrant card. 'We'd like to speak to Elizabeth Franklin please, on police business.'

'Is she expecting you?' the receptionist asked.

'No, she's not.'

'Please take a seat over there.' The woman pointed to the waiting area opposite where there were two black leather sofas and a coffee table with magazines on it.

After a few minutes, a woman in her mid-fifties with highlighted dark blonde hair hurried towards them, her face set and a pained expression in her eyes.

'I'm Elizabeth Franklin. What's happened, is it one of my parents?' She bit down on her bottom lip.

'No, we're not here about any of your family,' Whitney said in a reassuring tone.

'Thank goodness,' Elizabeth said, letting out a long sigh. 'At their age every time the phone rings I worry that something has happened to them.'

'I understand,' Whitney said. 'We'd like to talk to you somewhere quiet, if we may.'

'What is it about?' Elizabeth asked.

'Justin Robertson,' Whitney said.

Momentarily, the woman's face tightened before she composed herself. They followed her to a meeting room with a glass-topped round table surrounded by six chairs.

'How can I help you?' Elizabeth asked, once they were seated.

The woman gave the outward appearance of being in control, but the tight lines around her eyes gave her away. Whitney didn't need George to tell her that.

'We're investigating the murders of Anita Bailey and Jayne Kennedy,' Whitney said.

'I did see on the news that their bodies had been found on a building site, but I'm not sure how I can be of any help. I vaguely remember them from school and the fuss when they disappeared but that's about all. It was a lifetime ago.'

'How did you feel when you learnt of the girls' deaths?' Whitney asked, glancing at George who was scrutinising the woman's face.

'Obviously, when it was announced in the media I was sorry to hear about it, but they weren't friends of mine, so I'd be lying if I said it upset me at all.'

'We were informed that Anita and Jayne sold the drugs to Justin which led to his death. Can you confirm whether that was the case?'

She slumped forward slightly, a pained expression on her face. 'Yes, it's true.'

Was that why she wasn't concerned by the girls' deaths, because she held them responsible for what happened?

'Can you tell us more about Justin's relationship with Anita and Jayne?'

'He didn't have a *relationship* with them. They were in our year, but not the same form, and we didn't have anything to do with them. They weren't friends of ours.'

'Did Justin buy the drugs from them himself, or did someone buy them for him?'

'He bought them, there was no one else involved.' Her fists were clenched and rested on the table.

'Did you approve of what he did?'

'No. I was angry because I didn't want him to take anything, but he insisted it would be okay as we had friends who were already experimenting. We rarely argued but did over this. He'd been planning it a few weeks before his actual birthday and had bought the drug ten days before taking it. If only I'd tried harder to stop him, he might still be alive. I'll never forgive myself for that.'

Even after all this time.

'Did you take anything?' Whitney asked.

'No, I didn't. Justin understood and he didn't try to pressure me into it.'

'How did he know to buy the drugs from Jayne and Anita?'

'Everyone knew. It was common knowledge at school that if you wanted anything, they would be the ones to supply it.'

'Did the teaching staff know?'

'If they did they didn't do anything about it.'

'We also understand that another boy, Nigel Young, was selling at school.'

Elizabeth frowned. 'If he did then it wasn't common knowledge. I don't even remember him. There were six forms in the fifth year, each with over thirty pupils in them, so we didn't know everyone.'

'I'd like to go back to when you discovered Jayne and Anita had gone missing. You said you remembered the fuss … can you be more specific and explain exactly what happened and your reaction to it.'

'It wasn't long after Justin died, and I was operating on autopilot, but I do remember it was all anyone could talk about. At first they thought Jayne and Anita would come back, but they never did.'

'Did the police interview you about the girls going missing?'

'No. An officer spoke to each of the fifth form class groups individually and asked us to see them if we knew anything that would help. I don't know if anyone spoke to them. I didn't.'

'Did anyone mention to the police about the girls selling drugs at school?'

'I've no idea, it was something that was kept quiet, so most likely not.'

'What were your movements the day the girls disappeared? It was the 7th of May 1980.'

Elizabeth gave a small shrug. 'I don't know. All I remember is the police coming to see us the next day during class time.'

'Are you sure you can't remember what you were doing the day before,' Whitney pushed.

'I imagine I was at school during the day and at home after. I was still feeling lost because of Justin dying and I didn't go anywhere other than to school and then straight home to my bedroom. I'm sorry, Chief Inspector, but you're not only asking me to remember many years ago but you're focusing on something I've tried very hard to forget.'

'After Anita and Jayne disappeared and then didn't return, did it affect you at all?'

'To be truthful, I was the same as lots of others at school and very pleased they were no longer around because they weren't nice girls, and they were a constant reminder of what had happened to Justin. After they left there was a different atmosphere in the form. It was more relaxed and less confrontational and there was no bullying going on.'

That was the second time they'd heard that.

'You must've felt something when they went missing that was more than just relief at how the form now was. Deep down, did you hold them responsible for Justin's death?'

'Why would I? They weren't to know that he was going

to react to the drug like that. It was unforeseen and I bear no malice towards them. Then or now.'

'Yet you've just said that they were a *constant reminder*.'

'Okay, they were. But I didn't blame them.'

'How long was it between Justin dying and the girls going missing?' George asked.

Whitney nodded her approval at the question George had asked. Yet she'd kicked back when Brian tried it. She needed to change her mindset towards him, it wasn't fair.

'Four weeks.'

'Would you agree that at the time they went missing you were still in a state of grief?' George said.

'Undoubtably,' she said, nodding.

'And you'd gone back to school by then?'

'Yes, I had. I couldn't stay at home staring at the four walls of my bedroom. I needed something to take my mind off what had happened and going to lessons helped me do that.'

'Did anyone else have a bad reaction to drugs Anita and Jayne sold?' Whitney asked.

'Not that I know of.' Elizabeth shook her head.

'Is there anything else you can tell us which might help with our enquiry?' Whitney asked.

'I'm sorry, no. It was an awful time, obviously, when Justin died but, as I've told you, I didn't hold them responsible, and I certainly wasn't involved in their deaths.'

Whitney's ears pricked up. Elizabeth was already pre-empting a question linking her to the deaths, and it hadn't even been mentioned.

'But you don't have an alibi for when they went missing?'

'To repeat, I would have gone home after school because that's what I always did. My parents are now old and in care, so they won't be able to vouch for me. I'm sorry I can't help you any further.'

'According to Mr and Mrs Robertson, you stayed in contact with them until you left school and went to university. After that they didn't see or hear from you. Why is that?' Whitney asked.

'I wanted a clean break. The two years after Justin died were hard and the Robertsons acted as if he'd somehow return. They even kept his room untouched, apart from cleaning it every week. I couldn't take that intensity and needed to get away from them.' She plucked at the sleeve of her jacket, as if trying to remove fluff. There was none.

'If you do think of anything, please let me know.' Whitney handed her a card, and they all left the meeting room.

Once they'd returned to the car, Whitney turned to George. 'I don't know if you agree, but it seemed a case of *me thinks she doth protest too much* when she said she doesn't blame Anita and Jayne for Justin's death.'

'I did come to that conclusion, too. I'm impressed you used a quote from Shakespeare to illustrate your point.'

'I didn't know that's where it came from.' Whitney laughed. 'But holding them responsible doesn't mean she was involved in their deaths. She could have been covering her back because she was worried we might accuse her of being involved. When we get back to the station I'll ask someone to take a more in-depth look at Elizabeth Franklin and see if anything comes up requiring further investigation.'

Chapter 23

Whitney called the team to attention when they got back to the incident room. 'We've just interviewed Elizabeth Franklin. According to her, she doesn't hold a grudge against our victims for selling Justin the drugs as it wasn't their fault he'd had the fatal reaction. It was his decision to take them. Dr Cavendish and I both believe she was a little too insistent about this. Frank, I want you to do a thorough search into her, going back as far as you can.'

'Yes, guv,' Frank said.

'I'm also getting twitchy about the way the previous investigation was conducted. Ellie, you've gone through the files. What's your opinion?'

'Well …' she hesitated.

'This won't be held against you,' she said, to reassure the officer.

'It certainly wasn't very thorough. They assumed the girls had run away and didn't appear to follow up on any further leads. Like, the evidence from Kathleen Henderson, the girl who'd seen them talking to Reg Shaw outside the school. That was just ignored.'

'It's certainly strange. Who else was interviewed at the time?'

'The parents of both girls, and that's all, as far as I can tell,' Ellie said. 'Unless the interviews weren't recorded in the files.'

'You could be right. They may have carried out other interviews, including following up from what Kathleen Henderson had told them, but neglected to complete the paperwork. It was very different all those years ago. There were far less checks than there are for us now. They wouldn't have been bombarded with metrics or have KPIs to work with. Was there any mention of drugs, or Justin Robertson in there?'

'No, guv, but that's not surprising as our investigation pointed to the police not knowing about them dealing,' Ellie said.

'Good point,' she said.

'I think you're making allowances for them, guv,' Brian said. 'Surely there were protocols to follow, which would have meant the drugs business had been discovered. It wasn't bloody rocket science. We found out quickly enough.'

'You could be right. Who was the senior investigating officer on the case?' She gave a frustrated sigh.

'Inspector Malcolm Payne. He retired in 2005.'

'I was in the force then, but his name doesn't ring a bell,' she said. 'Ellie, find out where he lives, assuming he's still alive. Hopefully he's fairly local and we can have a chat with him about the investigation. He may be able to add something.'

'I'll look into it,' Ellie said.

'Brian, you can come with me.'

'Do we need permission to visit an ex-officer?' the sergeant asked.

Who from … Dickhead?

'This is my team and I decide,' Whitney said, coldly.

In her peripheral vision she caught sight of George frowning in her direction. She didn't need the psychologist to tell her she shouldn't have spoken like that to Brian.

'Guv,' Ellie called out, interrupting her thoughts. 'Inspector Payne lives in Upper Moreton.'

'That's not too far away. Text me his address and phone number and I'll give him a call. We can't just descend on him unannounced.'

She headed back to her office, and George followed.

'I'm glad you decided to take Brian and not me to see the inspector,' George said.

'It's an internal police matter, and not appropriate for you to attend, otherwise I would have.' Her phone pinged and she glanced at the screen. 'That's Ellie with the information I asked for. I'll give the inspector a call.'

'Would you like me to leave the room?' George asked.

'No, of course not. Just don't start singing and shouting while I'm talking.' She grinned.

'I've never done that before, so I'm hardly going to start now.'

'I realise that. I was attempting to lighten the mood.'

She keyed in the number and waited while it rang several times. She was about to end the call when it was answered.

'Hello.'

'Is that Malcolm Payne?'

'Yes.'

'I'm Detective Chief Inspector Whitney Walker from Lenchester CID, I'd like to come and see you about a current police enquiry, if that's okay.'

'Can you tell me what it's about?' he asked.

'We're investigating the murder of two teenage girls

who went missing in 1980. Their bodies were found recently. Your name is noted as being the officer in charge of the original enquiry into their disappearance. We'd really value your input and wondered if you could give us some background information.'

She didn't want him to think they were going to question his investigation. Not yet.

'I remember that case and I'd love to help. I miss the old days, it can get very dull around here,' he said, giving a chuckle.

'Are you available this afternoon by any chance?'

'Yes, we're in all day today.'

'I'll be bringing my sergeant. We should be with you around three.'

'Perfect. I'll make sure to have the kettle on. See you later.'

Whitney ended the call and turned to George. 'That's all set up. Hopefully he'll have something we can use.'

'How old is he?' George asked.

'I don't know, but assuming he retired at sixty then that puts him at mid-seventies. Why?'

'Just curious. I'm heading to work if you don't need me,' George said.

'We're all good here, thanks. I'll let you know how it goes with Payne.'

George left through the door leading to the corridor and Whitney returned to the incident room.

'Brian, I've arranged for us to visit Inspector Payne later. Ellie, what can you tell me about him?'

'I've accessed his police record and there's nothing on file to indicate he had any issues. As far as I can tell, his career was unblemished.'

'Thanks.'

She returned to her office and dealt with the pile of

admin on her desk, until two fifteen and then she returned to the incident room. Brian was at Ellie's desk hovering over her.

She walked over and could hear his voice booming out.

'You'll find that if you do use this database the results will come back much quicker and it will save you time. I'm an expert in it and can show you how it works.'

'Brian, are you ready?' she asked.

'Yes. I was talking to Ellie about different databases she could use in her research. It might speed things up.'

'Had you heard of these databases before, Ellie?'

'Yes, I have. But I prefer the one I use because of its functionality.'

'As long as we get the information in the end, that's the main thing,' Whitney said, trying to make light of it, but hoping Brian realised to leave Ellie to her own devices as she was the expert.

They left the station and drove through the city until reaching the country roads which lead to Upper Moreton.

'So you haven't come across the inspector at all in the past,' Brian said.

'I would have been a PC when he retired, so he must have been here, but I don't remember him. There are hundreds of officers in the force, and it's not possible to know everyone. Although there are some who have gone down in force history for all sorts of reasons. Some they'd probably wished they could forget.'

'True,' Brian said, grinning.

'We'll go in very laid-back and wanting Payne's help. I don't want to accuse him of handling the investigation poorly because he'll just clam up and we won't get anything of use out of him.'

'Got it.'

Upper Moreton was a large village on the outskirts of

Lenchester, and in its centre was a large, square green. Whitney remembered as a girl going with her parents to the annual fete which was held on there.

When they reached Payne's house, a small detached cottage with a thatched roof, Brian parked on the street. Before they'd even got to the front door, it was opened, and the inspector stood on the doorstep. He was tall, over six foot, and had a shock of white hair. He had a commanding presence. Weird that she didn't remember him.

'Mr Payne?' she asked,

'Yes. Come on in, Chief Inspector.'

'Please, call me Whitney.'

'And you must call me Malcolm.' He smiled. 'And you must be the sergeant,' he added.

'Yes, I'm Brian Chapman,' he said, holding his hand out and shaking the inspector's.

'Come on in. Ivy, my wife, is in the kitchen. Tea or coffee?'

'I'd love a coffee,' Whitney said. 'I have an absolute addiction to it.' Brian glanced at her, a frown on his face. 'Brian's new to the team. He doesn't know yet that I get exceedingly grumpy if I don't have a caffeine fix every couple of hours.'

'Ah ... so that explains it,' her sergeant said, laughing.

Good. They were putting Malcolm at ease. It was just what she wanted.

'We'll go into the sitting room.' He held open the door for them to enter, but before following them, he called out, 'Ivy our guests are here. Make it coffee all round, please.'

'I won't be a moment, dear,' his wife called back.

The sitting room was comfy and lived in. It had a traditional floral sofa and chairs, with matching curtains held open with dark red beaded tie-backs. There was a small fireplace with a beautifully patterned cast-iron surround. Piles of wood were stacked either side of it.

'This is a lovely house, Malcolm,' Whitney said. She'd love to be able to live somewhere like it.

'Thank you. We moved out here once I retired. It's a great village and the locals were very welcoming. We've made some great friends. Please, sit down and let me know how I can help you.'

Brian and Whitney sat on the sofa and Malcolm on one of the chairs. He moved the newspaper that was on there and placed it on the coffee table in the centre of the room.

'As I mentioned, we're investigating the murder of two girls whose bodies were found on Oak Tree Farm recently. Their names are Anita Bailey and Jayne Kennedy and they disappeared from their homes in 1980. According to the police files it was recorded that they'd run away. I wondered what you remembered of the case.'

He sighed and shook his head. 'It was a huge shock when I saw on the news about their bodies having been dug up. I'd be lying if I didn't admit to feeling guilty, but at the time everything had pointed to them running away. If only we'd have known ...'

'I'm not surprised you came to that conclusion. They were wayward girls. According to our investigation, they were bullies who sold drugs at the school.'

He frowned. 'Drugs? I don't recall that being mentioned, although it was a long time ago, and my memory isn't as good as it used to be.'

'It's my guess it wasn't recorded anywhere because the students at St Paul's kept it from you. It's only just come to light because the people we're interviewing are now adults, and not afraid to tell us what went on when they were at school.'

'If we'd have been informed, we'd definitely have investigated it.'

'Of course. The girls didn't leave notes for their family when they disappeared, didn't you think that was odd?' Whitney asked.

'Not at the time, no. We often found that runaways didn't let their parents know what they were doing. In the case of these girls we believed they'd seen the bright lights of London and took off. They wouldn't have been the first teenagers to do so.'

'Except we know that wasn't what happened.'

'Hindsight is a wonderful thing,' Malcolm said, sighing. 'But if I recall correctly, it wasn't the first time they'd run away.'

Whitney exchanged a glance with Brian. 'That's the first we've heard of this. It would certainly explain why your investigation took the route it did.'

Was she being too kind because she liked the man? She wasn't a stranger to being on the receiving end of a reprimand when an investigation had turned to crap.

'Indeed. It was why we assumed they'd run away and that they'd be back of their own accord.'

'How did you find out they'd run away before? Who told you?'

'You'll have to check the records. That should tell you.'

'That's the problem, there's hardly anything in there and certainly nothing pointing to them being habitual runaways.'

'I'm sorry, I don't remember.'

'Why didn't you follow up to see if the girls had returned?' Brian asked, his tone more accusatory than Whitney would have liked.

'We were busy due to being ridiculously understaffed. But you must remember that, Whitney. Were you in the force before I retired fifteen years ago? Your face is familiar.'

'I was, but our paths never crossed officially. I wasn't aware of staffing issues in CID at the time, but that's hardly surprising as I was only a PC.'

'Well, it was a difficult time and unfortunately the girls' disappearance was recorded as runaway and that's how it was left. We know now that's not what happened and—'

The sitting room door opened, and Mrs Payne walked in carrying a tray with cups of coffee and a cake.

'I made this yesterday,' she said as she placed the tray on the coffee table. 'I must've had a premonition you were coming. It's a Victoria sponge, who'd like a piece?' She picked up a knife from the tray and cut three slices, not waiting for their replies.

'Yes, please,' Whitney said.

'Me too,' Brian added.

Once Mrs Payne left the room, Whitney took a sip of coffee. It was instant but she could live with that, it was the caffeine she needed. The cake was exceptionally light and delicious.

'During your investigation did you come across a boy, Justin Robertson, who'd died from a reaction to a drug he'd taken a few weeks before?' Whitney asked.

He frowned. 'No, I don't recall that we did. Why is this relevant?'

'From our enquiries we've learnt that Anita and Jayne sold this particular drug to him.'

'Nothing like that came up in our investigation but, as I've already told you, we weren't aware of what they were doing.'

Whitney drew in a breath as she prepared herself to make life a little uncomfortable for the retired inspector. 'We've spoken to one of the students from St Paul's who saw the girls at lunchtime on the day they disappeared outside the school gate talking to a drug dealer. He was quite well-known in the area and had distinguishing tattoos, in particular an eagle on his neck. Did you investigate that?'

The inspector shifted awkwardly in the chair and glanced upwards and to the side. Whitney went on alert. She'd learnt from George that behaviour like that could mean someone was about to make up a story.

'As I recall, I'm not sure we did. Most likely it would have been because the girls didn't disappear until the afternoon so they'd been seen in school after their meeting with this man. My team isn't coming across well, but because we'd assumed they'd run away, we didn't look into what they were doing prior to their last sighting. They were in class during the afternoon only missing the last lesson, if I remember correctly. Obviously, it's many years ago and it's hard to know exactly, but I think I'm correct.'

Everything he said all seemed a little rehearsed. Had he been planning his response once he'd seen about the girls on the news, to cover his back, because of how crap his investigation had been?

'Is there anything you can think of that might help us with the investigation?' She leant forward and made eye contact.

He shook his head. 'I've told you everything I remember. Obviously, now we know they were murdered it changes everything but, unfortunately, nothing pointed to that at the time. I'm very sorry not to be of more use.'

She wasn't prepared to hang him out to dry as it wouldn't do any good in respect of them solving the crime. If he was anything like her, he'd be feeling mortified about having stuffed up so badly. But ... if something untoward had happened and she found out about it, she'd be back.

'You've helped us get it straight in our minds so thank you very much for that,' Whitney said.

They finished their coffee and cake and left. They headed down the short path and got back into Brian's car.

'Well. What do you think?' she asked him.

'For someone who can't remember anything from all those years ago, he certainly seemed to be remembering a lot, apart from why he thought the girls had run away in the past. I reckon he made that up so his investigation didn't look so bad.'

'My sentiments exactly. Call it gut instinct, or whatever, as long as you don't mention it to George, but nothing sits right. We need to look into the original investigation again and see what else we can find.'

Chapter 24

'Have you mentioned our holiday to your folks yet?' Ross asked George after they'd finished their meal and were sitting at her kitchen table talking.

'There's no need because we're going away after Christmas.' She picked up their plates and walked over to the sink, placing them on the side. She'd do the clearing up later.

'Are you still planning to see them on Christmas Day for lunch?'

'Yes, of course. It's a regular engagement. You can come with me if you wish although I don't recommend it.' It was bad enough that she had to endure the family Christmas lunch, but there was no need to inflict it on him.

'In that case, if you don't mind, I'm going to do the same as last year and spend it with my family. When will you be back?'

'I'll drive home late afternoon, early evening Christmas Day. I'll only have one glass of wine with my lunch, so driving won't be a problem.' She filled the kettle and took out two mugs to make them some herbal tea.

'Why don't you come and spend some time with my family once you're back, you could come over on Boxing Day. I know they'd love to see you.'

'Thank you for the invite but last year I spent the day with Whitney, and I may do the same again. She hasn't mentioned what she wants to do yet, but if she's going to be on her own, I want to spend the time with her. You can come along later.'

'That sounds good. Umm …' He hesitated. 'There is something else I'd like to speak to you about.'

She tensed. Was this heading where she thought it might be? Or was she just imagining it to be like the last time when he'd proposed and asked her to live with him? Only this time, she was more prepared.

'What is it?'

'I wondered—'

A knock at the door interrupted them. She glanced at her watch. It was seven-thirty and she wasn't expecting a visitor.

'I don't know who that is,' she said as she headed out of the kitchen and to the front door.

Standing on the doorstep was Whitney with a bottle of wine in her hand.

'I hope you don't mind me calling round on the off-chance. I wanted to speak to you about the interview with Malcolm Payne. I'd like your opinion, as an outsider.'

'Ross is here.'

Whitney's face fell. 'I thought I recognised the car parked in the street. Don't worry, I can go, we'll discuss it another time.'

'You don't have to leave. I'm sure Ross will be pleased to see you.'

They headed into the kitchen and Ross stood.

'Hi,' Whitney said, heading over and giving him a hug.

George wasn't envious of Whitney's open displays of affection, but she sometimes mulled over in her mind what it must feel like to be like that.

'I didn't know we were expecting guests,' Ross said, smiling.

'Neither did George,' Whitney said. 'I wanted to have a quick catch-up with her about developments on a case we're working on.'

'Over a few glasses of wine, no doubt,' he said, nodding at the bottle she was holding.

'Well, yes, there is that, too. You don't mind, do you?'

'No, of course not. I can go if you want to talk?'

'Don't be daft,' Whitney said. 'You can't leave because of me, I'd feel awful.'

'Why don't you two stay in the kitchen, and I'll go into the lounge and watch the telly.' He picked up his glass of wine from the table and headed towards the door.

'Are you *really* sure you don't mind?' Whitney said.

'It means I can watch the match. Leicester are playing Villa and George hates football.'

'Do you?' Whitney said, turning to George. 'I didn't know that.'

'Why would you, we've never discussed it?'

'True. I don't watch as much as I used to when my dad was alive. *Match of the Day* on a Saturday night was our treat. Mum was like you and not interested, unless it was something big like the cup final.'

'So, that's decided then,' Ross said as he headed out of the room, leaving them to it.

Whitney gave George the bottle of wine she'd been holding. 'I know you're going to say it needs to be chilled first, even though it did come from the fridge at the supermarket.'

'You're correct. I'll put it in the fridge. Have a glass of

this instead, I'm sure you'll enjoy it.' She poured a glass of red from the bottle they'd been drinking during their dinner and handed it to Whitney, who took a sip.

'Mmm. This *is* nice.'

'It's my preferred choice when we have lamb.'

'Now you tell me. If I'd known you were cooking, I'd have been here earlier. I had to stop for a burger on the way.' Whitney pulled out a chair and sat at the table. 'I won't keep you long, it's not fair on Ross, although now he's watching the match, he probably won't notice how long we take.'

'He understands about us having to work.' George sat opposite and had a sip of her wine. 'But …' She grimaced.

'What? Has something happened?' Whitney leant forward slightly, concern showing in her eyes.

'Not exactly … Ross was about to ask me a question when you arrived, and I suspect it might be to do with our relationship.'

Witney's hand shot up to her mouth. 'Oh, no, I'm really sorry. I'll go. That's far more important.'

'No.' George said, waving her hand. 'I *want* you to stay. It was perfect timing, to be honest because I still haven't worked out how I feel about our future together and don't wish to be rushed into making a decision I might regret.'

'Like before, you mean?' Whitney asked, arching an eyebrow.

'I admit that last time I might have made a mistake,' George agreed, nodding.

'You think?' Whitney raised her eyebrows. 'Well, you know my view.'

'Yes, I do. You've never held back in expressing it,' she said. 'We were also talking about Christmas. We're going skiing on the twenty-seventh, but I wondered if you'd like me to come around again on Boxing Day like we did last year.'

'Yes, that would be lovely. We can go and see Mum and Rob? I keep hoping Tiffany will appear so she can spend it with us, but the longer it goes on the less likely it's going to be. Although she has been very evasive when I discuss Christmas so, you never know, she might be planning a surprise. She'd love to see you on Boxing Day if she is here.'

'Ross may join us as well in the evening if you don't mind.'

'The more the merrier. You'll need some excitement after the trip to your parents for the annual Christmas lunch torture.'

Torture was the perfect way to describe it.

'Tell me about your interview with the retired inspector.'

'Malcolm Payne had an answer for everything and appeared too well prepared not to have known in advance that we would be calling on him. I also believe he might have lied to us about the girls having previously run away.'

'What was Brian's perspective on all of this?'

'He agreed with me that something wasn't sitting right. It was good to have him there and I'm getting used to his ways, even if they are different from Matt's. I just have to put to one side his relationship with Dickhead. I'm doing your *compartmentalising* stuff.'

'I'm glad to hear it. Are you sure about him knowing in advance? Couldn't he have guessed once he saw on the news about the girls' bodies being found?'

'Yes, I suppose so. When I phoned, he did act surprised and said he wanted to help as much as he could. But I'm not going to totally discount him being warned and if that was the case, who did it, and why?'

'Someone from the station who knew him from before might have contacted him. Especially as you requisitioned the old records. Who else was on the original investigation?'

'It's not clear as the files are so slim. I'll get Ellie on to it tomorrow morning, she'll be able to find out.'

'Did the inspector have enough time to get his story straight between the time you contacted him and when you arrived at his house?'

'I don't think so, unless he had a copy of the file with him, which is doubtful. So, he was either warned or for some reason he remembered the case. And if the latter, what is it that stuck with him, when you consider he would have investigated hundreds of cases during his time in CID?' Whitney paused. 'Unless he knew the investigation was lacking and that knowledge had stuck with him, and with us going to speak to him he wanted to cover his back. Whichever way we look at it, there's an issue.'

'But why go to all this trouble now, it's not like he's going to be disciplined, is it? Not after all this time.'

'No, he's not. But no police officer wants their work to be considered shoddy. Perhaps I'm overthinking and it could be just that.'

'Going back to the possibility of him being warned, could Chief Superintendent Douglas have mentioned it to him?'

'George, you're a genius. Payne was around for five years after I joined, and Douglas was definitely there.'

'If he did warn him, then why?'

'I'm not sure. Maybe he doesn't want to be associated with a sloppy police investigation so he's wanting Payne to have an answer for everything.'

'If you look into the investigation further, you might find that out.'

'I know we're trying to find the murderer of the girls, but this could also get Douglas reprimanded and I'm all for that, as you know.'

'Just be careful. You know what he's like and you don't want to make more of an enemy of him than he already is,' she warned.

'You're right. We'll leave Dickhead's input for now. The question is, where do we go from here? The inspector did say the girls had a history of disappearing, and that's why he'd immediately thought they were runaways. We need to check.' Whitney picked up her glass and finished the wine. 'I'm going now so the two of you can sort things out. How are you fixed for coming in to help?'

George exhaled a loud sigh, was she ready to face Ross again just yet?

'I'm not back in work until after Christmas, so can be available any time you need me.'

'Seriously? You mean you're not going to do anything?'

'I might do some preparation and work on my research, but that can all be done at home.'

'All right, tomorrow morning it is,' Whitney said as she walked out of the kitchen and called goodbye to Ross.

George closed the door behind Whitney and wandered through to the lounge, wondering what Ross was going to say. But she needn't have worried, he was on the phone.

Phew. A brief respite.

Chapter 25

Whitney looked out from her office into the incident room to check whether the team had arrived yet. They had, so she stopped what she was doing and walked through.

'Good morning, everyone. Brian and I went to visit Malcolm Payne yesterday and it's clear we need to look more into the previous investigation as there could be avenues that weren't investigated which could now assist us. Payne had an answer for everything I put to him and seemed too prepared. He could have been prewarned that we were unhappy with their work by someone who's still on the force. Ellie, which CID officers worked the case?'

'I only have Inspector Payne listed, plus the names of the uniformed officers who went to the school to speak to the pupils.'

'Damn. Okay, I want you to get me a list of CID officers who were working here at the time of the girls' disappearance and the cases they were assigned to.'

'Yes, guv,' Ellie said.

'Payne also said the girls had run away before and that's why they'd made their decision. When pushed on this he couldn't remember where they got that information and suggested we check in the records. When I explained there was nothing noted, he said it was a busy time, and they were stretched. Was he telling the truth? Are you able to track what cases were active during the time of the disappearance?'

'Yes, guv. I can look into it.'

'Leave that to me,' Brian said. 'Ellie can get on with investigating who was in CID.'

The door opened and George walked towards them. Whitney nodded in greeting. 'We've been going over the old investigation. Brian is finding out how busy the department was back then, and Ellie is looking into the team members. Our priority is to confirm whether Payne's version of events is accurate.'

'That should help,' George said.

'While they're doing that, I'd like to go back and visit the parents of the girls who went missing and find out if they did have a history of running away as Payne has suggested.'

'I'm ready whenever you are.'

'Before we go, Meena, phone Mr and Mrs Kennedy and find out if they're going to be in, and Frank you phone Mrs Bailey for the same. I don't want to turn up out of the blue, especially at this time of year.'

'Guv,' Doug said. 'I was wondering whether we should go back to visit the farm again with a view to discovering why it was used to dump the bodies. Was it convenience? Was it because the murderer knew the farm well and where best to hide a body? I know the farm workers have been interviewed but could it have been the farmer or his family?'

'They would hardly dig up the land if they knew the bodies were there, but you do make some valid points.

Once George and I have visited the families we'll go to the farm. It's on the same side of the city so will save time.'

'Guv,' Meena called out. 'Mr and Mrs Kennedy are at home all day if you want to call around.'

'Thanks. Frank?' she asked, noticing that he'd just ended his call.

'It went straight to answerphone, guv. She's gone away and won't be back until after Christmas.'

'Okay. We'll go to the Kennedys' and after that to the farm and have another chat with Anthony and see if he has anything to add, especially as we know about the drug connection. I'll take photos of the two dealers as he may recognise one of them.'

On the way to the Kennedys' house George turned to Whitney, who'd been quiet for most of the journey and concentrating on her phone.

'I'm glad to see you let Brian assist Ellie in the research,' she said.

Whitney looked up from her phone. 'I'm learning and, as you said, we're a team. I think it will all work out.'

'He appreciated it,' she reassured her friend.

'I'll take your word for it. I can't tell.'

'He needs your approval. Whether he's using his position on your team as a stepping-stone or not, he still needs to be utilised. You're his boss and he will be depending on you to give him a good reference if he wants to progress in the force. You're in the driving seat here.'

'I imagine he'll be going for inspector soon, once he's taken his exams. Hopefully then he'll move on to some other force. What I don't want is for him to suddenly be promoted to a higher position than me.'

'It's pointless worrying about something so far in the future. Concentrate on continuing to establish a good working relationship between the two of you instead, it will be a much more profitable use of your time.'

'Yes, oh wise one,' Whitney said, grinning in her direction.

'It's easier being an outsider looking on as it makes one more objective.'

'True,' Whitney said, nodding her head in agreement. 'Here we are. Park outside.'

They knocked on the door and Mrs Kennedy answered.

'Thank you for seeing us again,' Whitney said.

'We want to help any way we can,' she said as she ushered them into the sitting-room where Mr Kennedy was already seated.

'Have you heard from the coroner yet?' Whitney asked.

'They're returning Jayne to us in a few days. We're planning to hold her funeral in the new year, so as many of the family as possible can attend. There's a lot to do, and it isn't easy with Christmas being just around the corner.'

'We're here because we've spoken to the officer who ran the original investigation and who believed the girls had run away. At the time, were you told why they were so insistent on recording the girls as runaways?'

'No. We didn't see them very much after we initially reported the girls as missing and they came to the house to speak to us. Whenever we wanted to know anything it was down to us to contact them. We were never updated on their enquiries.' Whitney glanced at George and shook her head.

'The officer we spoke to, who has since retired, said that the girls had run away in the past, and that's why he assumed they'd done so again.'

Mrs Kennedy's eyes narrowed. 'I don't know where they got that idea from. Certainly not from us. Jayne had never run away before. *Never.*'

'Is it possible that Jayne and Anita had decided to run away before but changed their minds before you'd even realised? Someone who knew about that could have informed the police,' Whitney said.

'I suppose so, but that's unlikely. They did play truant from school and we were called in to see the headmistress about it several times, but … where did he get the idea the girls had run away in the past? You should ask him.' Her eyes filled with tears and she pulled out a tissue from her sleeve and dabbed them away.

'We did, but unfortunately there's no record of who informed him and he doesn't remember. Could Anita have run away in the past and the officers assumed it was both of them?' Whitney asked, the lines around her eyes tight as if she was trying to hold back from blurting out about the utter incompetence of the CID back then.

'I suppose so, but you'll have to speak to Anita's parents.'

'Unfortunately, Mrs Bailey is away until after Christmas. But we will ask her when she's back.'

'I don't understand why they would have said that,' Mr Kennedy said, speaking for the first time. 'They knew we were putting up all the posters and we didn't think they'd run away. Surely, they would have said something to us then.'

'Did you ask for any help from the police regarding the posters and all the publicity?' Whitney asked.

'Yes, I phoned and spoke to an officer, I can't remember his name, but he said the police couldn't help because they were busy with other cases. It was like they couldn't care less about Jayne.'

'Do you remember whether you spoke to Inspector Payne at all during the investigation?'

'The name does ring a bell,' Mr Kennedy said, nodding. 'Do you remember?' he asked his wife.

'I think we might have spoken to him,' she agreed. 'But I can't be sure.'

'Thank you for seeing us, we won't take up any more of your time. We'll let you know how we get on.'

'Yes, please do,' Mrs Kennedy said, tears returning to her eyes which she blinked away. 'This might sound strange but you finding Jayne has helped us, because always at the back of our minds we wondered where she was and why she hadn't been in touch with us. We even thought she might have had an accident and lost her memory. We wondered if she had a family of her own. All those questions go around and around in your head but are impossible to answer. But now we know the entire time she'd been buried somewhere close.'

'I understand exactly what you mean,' Whitney said.

'If only you'd been in charge at the time Jayne went missing, things might have turned out differently.' She let out a sob, and Mr Kennedy put his arm around her.

'Come on, Nancy. We can't change what's happened, but at least we have answers.'

'Yes,' she said sniffing.

'We'll see ourselves out and as soon as we have any information, we'll make sure to tell you,' Whitney said.

Mr Kennedy nodded in their direction as they left the room and headed back outside.

'This is puzzling,' George said as they climbed into the car.

'Yes, the plot thickens. It's looking as though the girls being runaways in the past was a fabrication, unless the other parent can confirm it.'

'Is there any way you can get in touch with Mrs Bailey?' George asked.

'According to Frank, she's away until after Christmas but we might be able to trace her mobile number and call her that way. I'll get on to that when we get back to the station, after we've been to the farm.'

Chapter 26

George declined to take Whitney's shortcut to the farm when she'd suggested it, saying it would be too muddy. Whitney didn't insist as she had initially done with Brian as she didn't want to be the cause of the new car getting wrecked, especially if they ended up going over lots of potholes.

When they arrived, George parked outside the farmhouse behind an old Land Rover and they went to the front door and knocked. There was no reply and Whitney knocked again just as an old man answered.

'Hello, I'm Detective Chief Inspector Walker and this is Dr Cavendish, is Mr Gibson in?'

'That's me.'

Whitney frowned. 'It's your son we'd like to speak to,' she said, remembering that he'd mentioned his father living with them.

'He's on the farm somewhere. Come inside and I'll see if I can contact him on the radio,' the old man offered.

'Thanks. We're happy to wait.'

He opened the door fully and led them through into the large kitchen where they sat down at the table. He picked up a walkie-talkie and radioed to his son.

'Hello, Tony. The police are here to speak to you.'

'I'll be at least twenty minutes. I've got a problem with a fence which needs urgent attention.' His son's crackling voice came through. The old man looked at Whitney.

'Yes, that's fine,' she said, nodding. If they didn't speak to him today it would mean another visit out here and they didn't have the time.

'They'll wait for you,' old Mr Gibson said, signing off. 'Can I get you something to drink while you wait?'

'Coffee would be lovely,' Whitney said, and George agreed.

The old man shuffled over to the machine in the corner, took three mugs from the Welsh dresser which stood at the end of the kitchen, and poured one for them all.

'I understand you were running the farm in 1980,' Whitney said, when he came back with a tray, which he set down on the table.

'That's right. My parents moved into one of the farm cottages in 1975 and I lived here in the main house with my family. My father had taken a back seat and left me with the day-to-day operations, in much the same way as I have with Tony.'

'We're trying to ascertain why the farm was used to bury the girls all those years ago and hoping that you might be able to help. Can you remember, was there a regular flow of people visiting the farm in those days?'

The old man nodded. 'There were the farm workers, our friends and relatives but also part of the farm included a public right of way, still does, which meant there were always strangers walking through. Especially in good weather.'

'Yes. We were aware of that.'

'And, of course, there was the clay pigeon club who used the land on a weekend.'

Whitney went on alert, regular visitors to the farm would be more likely to work out a place to bury bodies as they had opportunity to scrutinise the place without being suspected of doing anything untoward.

'Can you tell me more about this club?' she asked.

'They met every Sunday morning for three hours and paid me monthly for using the land.'

'Do you still happen to have details of the club?' she asked on the off-chance, although how likely would that be after all these years?

'Yes, I've kept all of my records, but they might be hard to access.'

As much as she wanted to, she refrained from punching the air … it was hardly the behaviour of a DCI. She did glance across at George and give a small smile, though.

'Please could you look?'

'They're probably in the office with all my old paperwork.'

'Let's go,' she said, anxious to see what he'd got.

They followed him out of the kitchen and into the office. On one side, covering the entire wall, there were box files stacked high on shelves.

'Oh, goodness. How on earth can you find anything in here?' George asked.

'In the old days we kept everything in boxes. Now Tony uses the computer, but we've still kept all of the old records.'

'We're looking for 1980,' Whitney said.

'Everything relating to that time will be over here,' he said as he headed over to the shelves on the left. He stared at the boxes for a few seconds and then pointed to one at the top. 'Up there,' he said.

'I'll get it.' George reached for the small ladder resting against the wall and leant it against the shelf. She climbed up several rungs, until she could reach the top, and lifted up the box labelled 1980, and handed it to the old man. Thank goodness for George because if it was left to Whitney, she might not have been able to reach.

Mr Gibson rested the box on the desk and rummaged through. 'Here's my little receipt book.' He handed it to Whitney. 'Come to think of it, I think the group were your lot.'

Whitney frowned. 'My lot?'

'Police.'

Whitney's skin prickled as it usually did when new evidence came to light. 'Talk me through how this arrangement worked.'

'It wasn't complicated. The man who ran the club paid me cash monthly and I gave him a receipt.'

'Can you remember his name?'

The old man paused for a while. 'He had a nickname. I think it was Digger. No, it was *Dodger*.'

The name meant nothing to her, but they could soon check once they were back at the station.

'Was Malcolm Payne one of the club members?' she asked, wondering if the inspector had been part of the group.

'The name doesn't ring a bell, but I didn't have much to do with the rest of them.'

'How many members belonged to the club?'

'There were usually ten regulars and occasionally others would join them.'

'Did you check on them every week?' Whitney asked, wondering how he knew exactly.

'I would watch, if I wasn't busy, and sometimes shot a few clays with them. Not very often, though.'

'Is there anything else you have relating to the club?'

'No, just this little receipt book as they paid me cash.' He glanced away.

'We don't care about whether you paid tax on it,' she said, assuming that was the reason for the guilty look. 'But I would like to take the receipt book away with me as it might help with our enquiries.'

'Okay,' he said.

'How long did the club use the farm?' she asked.

'1980 was their last year.'

'Why did they stop?' Whitney asked.

'I don't know.'

'That's no problem, you've been extremely helpful. We'll get going now.'

'Don't you want to wait and speak to my son?'

'We'll call back another time, thank you.'

'Do you think it might be something to do with the clay pigeon club?'

Whitney didn't want him to think the police were involved in the murders. 'No, but they might be able to help, if they saw anyone hanging around or acting suspiciously while using the public footpath. They were trained in observation.'

'Yes, that makes sense,' he said, nodding.

'Thank you again.'

They followed him out of the office and back into the kitchen where she finished the remainder of her coffee and placed her mug on the table. They then left the farmhouse and went to the car.

'I want to know more about this clay pigeon club. I

hate to say it, but from what we've now learnt, combined with everything else, it's pointing to police involvement in these deaths.'

Chapter 27

I can't bear this for much longer it's making me ill. Every time the phone rings or there's someone at the door my heart is in my mouth as I expect it to be the police coming here accusing me of killing those girls. I would deny it, of course, but if they traced it back to me they'd have to have found strong evidence. But there wasn't any. I'm being silly.

It crossed my mind it would be best if I gave myself up and told them everything that happened on that dreadful day, but what would be the point? It wouldn't change anything. It wouldn't bring the girls back. It was an accident which happened decades ago.

I haven't slept for days since seeing that news report. I'll be resorting to sleeping pills soon as I'm exhausted and can hardly function.

I just wish it would all go away, I'm too old to be upset like this. Friends and family are noticing that there's something wrong and I've fobbed them off with excuses.

How much longer will this go on for? Surely, the police have better things to be investigating than something which happened a lifetime ago. The police are always complaining about a lack of resources, so they shouldn't be wasting any on something that happened so long ago.

Every day I'm glued to the news on the television and radio, just to see if there's anything pointing to me. But so far there isn't. I keep telling myself that soon it will be over, and that they'll give up their search. That I should just get on with my life and pretend it didn't happen.

At my age, prison isn't an option. It would kill me.

Chapter 28

Whitney and George walked into the incident room and she closed the door behind them. She was going to be bending the rules slightly, as she knew she should be speaking to Clyde first, but as the team had already been working on the case, and all of their suspicions had been aroused, she decided against it. This was something they needed to get totally straight before anyone was accused, because once they'd got that far there, was no turning back.

Whitney had no idea how Clyde was going to react. She might want a cover-up, or she might want to get it all out in the open. Either way, she'd want absolute proof and that's what Whitney planned to have for her.

'Attention, everyone.' She paused for a moment until they were all focused on her. 'We potentially have something big. Something that stays within these four walls until such time as I say otherwise.'

You could hear a pin drop as everyone stared in her direction.

'What is it, guv?' Frank asked.

'We don't now believe that the girls had run away in the past and, Frank, I want you to find the mobile number for Mrs Bailey and seek confirmation from her.'

'I'm on to it, guv' Frank said. 'What else is there? That isn't enough for all this *cloak and dagger* stuff.' He did quote marks with his fingers.

'If you give the guv a chance, she'll tell us,' Doug quipped.

Frank scowled at him. 'You give her a chance, and then—'

'Boys ... give it a rest.' She glared at them. 'Frank, you were right. In itself that isn't enough, although it did put us on alert. At the farm we met old Mr Gibson, Anthony's father. He told us that they allowed a clay pigeon shooting club to use a field close to where the bodies were buried. They met there every Sunday morning and paid monthly, until the end of 1980.'

'And?' Frank said. 'Come on, guv, stop spinning this out for effect.'

She gave a hollow laugh. 'Not intentional I can assure you. The clay pigeon club was run by none other than ... the Lenchester police.'

'Fuck,' Frank said.

'My sentiments exactly,' Whitney said.

'Do you think whoever dumped the bodies was a copper?' Doug asked.

The question on everyone's lips.

'We don't know, and I don't want to make any assumptions as we need clear-cut evidence. This is what we're going to do. First, Ellie, I want you to look into the clay pigeon club. The person in charge, who made the arrangements and paid Mr Gibson, was known as Dodger. The club might have entered contests or there could be something in the force newsletters from back then. There were about ten regulars who shot each week, and they were occasionally joined by others. Anything you can find, however small, let me know. Doug and Meena can help you, instruct them on what you'd like them to do.'

With Matt gone she wanted Ellie to be more assertive as she didn't have him to lean on all of the time. It would do her good.

'Yes, guv,' Ellie said, hesitating slightly.

'Before you start, where are you with that list?'

'There were fifteen officers in CID in May 1980 and I've emailed you their names, guv.'

She hadn't checked her email in a while. 'Any names you recognise?'

'Only Inspector Payne.'

Damn, that ruled out Douglas.

'Meena and Doug, go through the list of CID officers and see what you can turn up.'

'Brian, what about the cases they were working, any joy?'

'It was harder than I thought, but from what I can tell they weren't overly busy. I managed to track down over-time records, and there weren't many hours claimed.'

'That's useful to know. I can't emphasise enough that we've got to be careful. We can't go around accusing one of our own until we've done a thorough investigation, and some.'

'If Payne insisted that the girls had been runaways in the past and he lied about how busy they were at the time, do you suspect him of being involved?' Brian asked.

'I'm not sure. He could have been, or it might have been other officers and he was trying to protect them, for some reason. At the moment it's all supposition. Let's wait to see if Frank is able to contact Anita's mother.'

She glanced over to the older officer who had his phone to his ear. She waited until his conversation finished.

'Guv,' he called out. 'I've just spoken to Mrs Bailey and she said that Anita hadn't run away before.'

'Thanks, Frank.' She turned to Brian. 'Now we have our answer. I want you to do some digging into Payne when he was serving. See what you can find, however small. I'll have to speak to the super about this, but not until we have something concrete to tell her. Rumour and guesswork won't hack it.'

'Agreed, guv. Leave it with me.'

'Thanks, Brian. I'll be in my office with George if you need me.'

They went to her office and she closed the door behind them, gesturing at George to sit at the table where they couldn't be seen.

'This could develop into a huge scandal,' George observed.

'You're telling me. I just hope Brian doesn't leak this to Dickhead. We've got to play it very carefully and I don't want him to accuse us of not running the investigation properly, especially as he might think Clyde should have been informed already.'

'Should she have?'

'I'm in two minds. On the one hand everyone knows how the investigation is progressing, on the other, we are talking about possible corrupt police practice. But I've made my decision on how it's going to be tackled and am prepared to back myself, if it comes to it.'

That thought had only just come into her head, and she wished it hadn't. She had enough to worry about without adding to it.

'I'm sure Brian won't inform Douglas. As I've said before, he wants to be a valuable part of the team. When you asked him to research into the inspector his chest puffed out slightly and the expression on his face was of someone eager to please. The untrained eye might not have noticed.'

'Well, it escaped my notice. I hope you're right because it wouldn't look good if Dickhead found out before the super.'

'The fact that the inspector has retired, does that matter?'

'No. It will still be treated in the same way, which is why we can't accuse one of our own without good reason. But I'm jumping the gun here. First, we don't know if he had anything to do with the clay pigeon shooting club, or if the club was involved.'

'I understand. Do you need me here any longer?' George asked.

'Why? Is there somewhere you want to go?'

'I want to go into the city to buy a few items I need for our skiing trip, and then go home to start sorting out all of my gear.'

'We can manage without you and I'll get in touch if you're needed. If it does involve police officers, this will blow up very quickly. I want to get this sorted before Christmas if possible.'

George left and Whitney returned to the incident room just as Ellie was heading towards her.

'I've got something for you. I've traced the clay pigeon shooting club.'

Whitney's heartbeat quickened. That was quick.

'And?' Whitney anxiously moved from foot to foot.

'Dodger was the nickname for Sergeant Dodgson, he retired from the force thirty years ago.'

'I've never heard of him, but—'

'That's not all,' the officer interrupted. You were right

about them entering contests. I found the results of one they entered in March 1980, in Birmingham and … Inspector Payne was on the team.'

'Stop what you're doing,' she said to the team. 'Ellie has discovered that Malcolm Payne was a member of the clay pigeon shooting club.'

'Does that mean we've got ourselves a bent copper?' Frank said.

'That's what we need to find out. We need to find a reason why Payne would be involved with the girls and their murders. What benefit did it have for him when they disappeared? I'm going to see the super as this is now above my pay grade. We can't question Payne and accuse him without her permission. Ellie, I want you to continue investigating the shooting club. Could Payne have been working with someone else? Were there any other officers involved and, if so, how many? We have no idea how big this is going to be.'

'Yes, guv. I'm on to it.'

Whitney left and headed down the corridor on her way to Clyde's office.

'Guv, hang on a minute.' She turned around at the sound of Brian's voice.

'What is it?'

'I've just found something that's going to blow this case apart.'

Chapter 29

Reeling from Brian's discovery, Whitney didn't take the lift to the super's office, and instead took her time, going over in her mind *what* she was going to say, and *how* she was going to say it. She had no idea what the super's reaction was going to be. Whitney was in uncharted territory and, for once, she was glad the buck didn't stop with her.

Before she'd come to a decision about how to approach the disclosure, she'd arrived at the office. After counting to ten, she sucked in a calming breath and knocked on the door, half-hoping that the super wasn't there, or was too busy to see her. Anything to give her a few more moments to prepare.

'Come in,' Clyde called.

It wasn't to be.

She opened the door and stepped into the office as the super glanced up from the files in front of her. Clyde placed the pen in her hand on the desk and looked directly at Whitney.

'We've got an issue, ma'am, needing your immediate attention.'

The super's expression remained the same, calm and unfazed. She couldn't be less like Jamieson if she'd tried. He'd have gone all blustery and demanded to know exactly what had been going on, and in the process assumed it was all Whitney's fault. And she didn't need to think about Jamieson at a time like this.

'Sit down, Whitney, and explain to me the situation.'

She sat on the chair in front of the super's desk, resting her hands on her lap. She had to appear relaxed, composed, and in control. 'During our investigation into the bodies dumped on Oak Tree Farm, we have discovered that Inspector Payne, who led the initial enquiry into the girls' disappearance and has since retired, may have been involved.'

The super stared at her for a few seconds, clearly processing what she'd been told. 'That's a heavy accusation to make against an officer. What evidence do you have?'

'I agree, ma'am, and it isn't one I'm making lightly, I can assure you of that.'

'I didn't believe you were, Whitney. I already know you well enough to realise that you're only here because you've got to the stage of requiring my involvement.' The super leant forward slightly, giving Whitney her full attention.

'Payne has lied to us regarding several aspects of the investigation. Also, during 1980, when the bodies were dumped, the farm was used by a clay pigeon shooting club run by the Lenchester police force. Inspector Payne was a member.'

'Okay.' The super nodded. 'I agree it's looking suspicious, but I'm not sure that it's enough to blame him.'

Not yet she didn't.

'I've saved the best bit until last,' Whitney said, shaking her head.

'Whitney, this isn't a play, I really don't like all the theatrics.'

'Sorry, ma'am. I was leading up to it because ...' Her voice fell away. 'Because it's not pleasant to have to accuse one of our own.'

'I agree. Now tell me the rest.'

'The dead girls sold drugs to a boy who died, as you know. The mother of the dead boy, Peggy Robertson ... it turns out that she's Malcolm Payne's cousin.'

Brian had been right. This totally blew the case apart.

'Shit. This is bad.' Clyde muttered, as she leant back in her chair and looked at Whitney, while shaking her head.

'Yes, ma'am, it is.' Whitney exhaled a long breath. She hadn't enjoyed telling the super one little bit, even if it did mean the case was going to be solved.

'When you interviewed Payne, did he appear guarded, as if he expected you to accuse him?' the super asked.

'On the contrary, he was helpful and calm but that's possibly because he had no idea what the extent of our enquiry was, or what we'd unearthed.'

'You do know everything has to be done by the book. What do you plan to do next?'

'With your permission, I'm going to take DS Chapman and bring Mr and Mrs Robertson, the parents of the dead boy, in for questioning. It's pointing to them being involved with Payne. They're elderly and will be treated gently. I'll ask Dr Cavendish to observe the interview as she specialises in body language and will be able to assist. She'll let me know, as the interview progresses, if there are any telltale signs we can use to extract further information.'

'That's a good idea. I understand now why you wanted a budget to include using her when necessary. I'd like to meet her when you have a spare moment.'

'Thank you, ma'am. We'd have solved far fewer cases

without her input. We have to be careful as we don't want them to warn Payne of our suspicions, so before the Robertsons are allowed home, following their interviews, I think we should bring him in. That way, they won't be able to warn him.'

'I agree, that's the best way forward. Remember, take it steady, make sure everything is done by the book and keep me informed. It might work in your favour if you can get Payne to come in voluntarily, on the pretext of needing his help. Update me after you've interviewed the Robertsons, and before Payne comes in.'

'I could say we need him to check some photos. I'll see how it goes.'

Whether he'd agree to come in immediately remained to be seen. If he did it would make things much easier, if he didn't then she'd have to insist.

'Chief Superintendent Douglas needs to be informed about this,' Clyde said, her voice reticent.

Whitney's heart sank. He was bound to try to interfere, which was just what she didn't need.

'Do we need to do that *straightaway* as we don't have anything concrete yet?'

'I'm sorry, but we can't cut any corners, or it could blow up in our faces. He won't interfere, I'll make sure of it.'

If only Whitney could be certain. But she didn't have time to dwell on it, there was work to be done.

'Thank you, ma'am.'

What else could she say?

'I'm relying on you to ensure this is handled with the utmost care and diplomacy. Don't let me down.'

Whitney returned to the incident room and the moment she entered, all eyes were on her.

'Brian, have you told the rest of the team about Payne

and Mrs Robertson?' she asked before discussing their plans for dealing with Payne.

'I'd just this moment finished, guv.'

'So, Payne's definitely involved in the deaths,' Frank said. 'Everything points to it. Nice work finding out about her cousin, Sarge.'

'Thanks, Frank. Any one of us could have discovered it, it just happened to be me.'

Whitney stared in his direction. Those words spoke volumes to her about how he was going to integrate into the team.

'Let's not get too carried away,' she said. 'We don't know for sure. I've spoken to the super and she's agreed that we first interview Justin Robertson's parents. Brian, you and I are going to visit them and bring them in for questioning. What's most important is that we keep them together, to prevent either of them contacting Payne. We don't want him to get wind of what we've discovered.'

'Yes, guv. I'll grab my jacket.'

'I'll be with you shortly as I'm going to call Dr Cavendish. If possible, I want her observing our interviews as she will be able to feed us any useful insights she makes, and guide us.'

'Are you sure that's necessary? They're two elderly people, the interviews won't be difficult,' Brian said, frowning.

'Trust me on this. Dr Cavendish will notice the minutest of changes in their faces and body language, which we wouldn't pick up on. I'm not saying that we wouldn't eventually get the information we need, but her input will speed up the process. She's worth her weight in gold.'

'Okay, I'm convinced.'

Whitney returned to her office, pulled out her phone and pressed the speed dial for George.

'Whitney?'

'We've broken the case wide open. Brian found out that Justin Robertson's mum is Malcolm Payne's cousin.'

'That's excellent. Well done.'

'I know you're probably not even home yet, but I really need you back at the station. We're going to bring in Mr and Mrs Robertson and I'd like you to observe the interview. Is there any chance of you being here within the hour?'

'No problem, I'll turn around and will be with you shortly,' George said.

'Thanks. I'm not looking forward to what's going to happen. I want to solve the case, obviously but it's never pleasant when an officer is involved. Can you imagine what's going to happen when the media gets hold of the story? All hell will let loose.'

Chapter 30

They pulled up outside of the Robertsons' house and Whitney turned to Brian.

'Leave the talking to me when we're with them.'

'Yes, guv. I'm now fully acquainted with your *rules.*'

She bristled, then noticed the grin on his face.

'I'm glad to hear it,' she replied, nodding her approval. 'The plan is to get them to come willingly, without alerting them to there being anything wrong. When we get them back to the station, we'll put them in different rooms and interview them separately.'

'How are you going to do that without them suspecting they're there for other reasons? Won't they think it strange?'

'I've been thinking it through and decided that I'll ask for their help with some photographs and say we don't want them to influence each other with the identifications. If that doesn't work, we'll have to come up with something else. We mustn't forget that they're elderly, so we can't push them too far. Which is why we're going to take a softly, softly approach. Let's go.'

They walked up the short path and she knocked on the front door. Mrs Robertson answered after a few seconds.

Her eyes widened. 'Hello, Inspector. We weren't expecting to see you again.'

She appeared nervous. Although Whitney didn't want to read too much into that, because people were often wary of the police.

'We're still working on the case of the two young girls who were found buried on the farm, and we wondered if you could help us. Is Mr Robertson here?' she asked, smiling, hoping to relax her.

'Yes, we both are.'

'We've got some photos at the station that we'd like you both to look at, if you don't mind. We will take you and bring you back once you've seen them.'

'Can't we do it here?'

'Unfortunately not. Everything we have is on computer. You know what all this modern technology is like,' she said shaking her head. 'I'm hopeless with it.'

'Oh, yes, we understand. It all goes way over our heads, too.'

Exactly what Whitney had been counting on.

'I think it does for everyone apart from kids,' Whitney said.

'Okay, I'll get Kenneth and we can go.'

'Thank you, we really appreciate you taking the time to help us,' Whitney said.

They waited while the couple got their coats and followed them to the car.

'It's nice to get out,' Mrs Robertson said. 'We've been stuck inside recently because of the weather. It's too dangerous and I don't want to go slipping and sliding on icy paths. I broke my hip from a fall last year and haven't fully recovered. That's why I use this stick.' She held up a brightly patterned cane.

'You'll be able to see our new station and maybe have a coffee in the cafeteria.' Brian suggested.

Whitney nodded her approval at his comment. It helped towards not alarming them, although if it turned out they were involved and then arrested, it wasn't going to happen. She doubted they would be in the position to charge them at this stage, though.

The journey didn't take long, and Mrs Robertson chatted non-stop for most of the way while her husband remained silent. Nerves? They affected people differently.

Once they arrived at the station, Whitney signed them in and took them towards the interview rooms.

'What we're going to do, if you don't mind, is ask you to go into separate rooms so we can show you some photos individually. That way you won't be influenced by each other and then if you both recognise who you're shown it makes the identification more solid.'

The couple exchanged a glance. Mrs Robertson's pupils were dilated. She was panicking.

'I'm not sure,' Mr Robertson said, hesitating.

'It will be fine, and shouldn't take too long,' Whitney said gently. 'Brian, you can take Mr Robertson to interview room one and I'll take Mrs Robertson to interview room two. Then arrange for coffee and cake for both of them. I'm assuming you would like something?' she asked, looking from one to the other.

Whitney figured they wouldn't get suspicious if they were being offered something to eat and drink. It didn't stop her from feeling guilty about deceiving them, though.

'That would be lovely,' Mrs Robertson said, relief in her voice.

'Thank you,' her husband said.

After leaving Mrs Robertson on the pretext of arranging for some technical help, Whitney went to the incident room to see if George had arrived.

She had.

'Great, you're here. Who do you suggest we interview first?'

'I'd go with Mrs Robertson as, from memory, she was more open than her husband. She's more likely to give you the information you need, as I suspect she may speak before she thinks which will go in your favour.'

'Good point, although she's definitely wary about being here. We'll try to keep this as short as we can because we have to interview him as well and I don't want to leave him alone for too long. I told them they were going to be looking at photos, so I'll show them the drug dealers first and then the victims. I doubt they'll recognise the dealers, but that doesn't matter.'

After George had gone into the observation room, Whitney waited for Brian. He arrived with a coffee and piece of cake for Mrs Robertson. Whitney got a whiff of coffee as he got closer. She should have asked for one for herself.

'I've taken the same into Mr Robertson,' he said.

'Good, that should keep him busy for a while. I'm going to need you to put the photos up on the screen when required as you're better with the equipment than I am. Also, remember, we're taking it steady and there's to be no aggressive questioning.'

'I know, guv. We've already discussed this.'

She opened the door and they walked in.

'Thanks for waiting, Mrs Robertson.'

Brian placed the plate and mug on the table in front of her. 'You'll love this cake,' he said. 'I make a point of having a slice every day.' He glanced at Whitney and gave a tiny nod.

She got the message.

'Thank you,' Mrs Robertson said.

'I'm going to record our interview as it saves me having to take notes,' Whitney said. She leant over and pressed the recording equipment. 'Interview on December twenty-second. Those present: Detective Chief Inspector Walker, Detective Sergeant Chapman. And please state your name for the recording.'

'Peggy Robertson,' the woman said as she leant right over towards the equipment.

'No need to do that, Mrs Robertson, as the recorder will pick up all of our voices from where we are,' Whitney reassured her.

'Oh, sorry, I didn't realise.'

'We have some photos to show you which we're going to put up on the screen over there.' She pointed at the wall and nodded to Brian to load the first one which was of Reg Shaw the drug dealer. 'Do you recognise this man?'

Mrs Robertson opened her handbag, which was resting on her lap, and took out a pair of glasses. After putting them on, she stared at the screen for a few seconds, finally shaking her head. 'No, I'm sorry. I've never seen him before.'

'He's the drug dealer Anita Bailey and Jayne Kennedy worked for. It was one of his drugs they sold to Justin and caused him to die. Please could you take another look, just to make doubly sure that you don't recognise him.'

Mrs Robertson stared at it again, for even longer this time. 'No. I definitely haven't seen him before.'

'Do you recognise these girls?' Brian put up photos of the victims. 'Do you remember seeing them before?'

'Yes, she does,' George said in her ear. 'Her shoulders

went rigid and her eyes flickered with recognition. Although she could have seen their faces on the news, as the media has been showing them.'

'No, I've never seen them before.' Mrs Robertson's tone was adamant.

'She's lying. She didn't blink once while she was talking to you, and now she's blinking furiously. When she displayed recognition previously it can't have been from seeing them in the media, or she wouldn't be behaving like this.'

And that's why George was so invaluable to them. It was a shame Brian couldn't hear what Whitney could.

'Mrs Robertson, I believe you do know these girls and that you have seen them before.' Whitney's tone was firm.

She glanced quickly at Brian, who was frowning. Probably because she'd done exactly what she'd said they wouldn't do and been aggressive.

'No, I haven't … I don't know them … I don't remember.' Her body tensed and her eyes reflected panic.

'Your body language is telling us otherwise. Think very carefully. Have you seen these girls before?'

'I might have. They were friends with Justin. Yes, that's it. They were friends. He must have brought them round to the house sometime, or we might have seen them when we were out. Or at school. Definitely. That's it.'

'She's making this up,' George said. 'You can see by the way she's glancing up and to the right.'

'Mrs Robertson,' Whitney said softly, deciding now to take a gentler approach as she didn't want to scare the woman into clamming up completely. 'I know this is painful for you, but I believe there is something that you want to tell us about this.'

The elderly woman slumped in her chair, her breathing raspy and laboured.

'Are you okay, Mrs Robertson?' Brian said. 'Would you like some water?'

'I'm fine, thank you.' She sat more upright and sucked in a breath. 'I'll tell you. I've thought of nothing else over the years and it will be good to get it off my chest.'

Whitney tensed in anticipation. Was she going to admit to killing the girls and tell them how Payne was involved?

'Okay, go ahead. There's no rush. We can stop for a breather any time you want to,' Whitney said hoping her words would help the woman open up to them.

'I have seen those girls before, you were right. I blamed them for what happened to Justin and wanted them to pay. He was our only child. My pride and joy. I loved him more than anything in the whole world and they took him away from us, with their stupid, horrible drugs.' Her eyes brimmed with tears and she opened her bag and pulled out a tissue, wiping them away.

'Take your time,' Whitney said gently.

'But it all went wrong. Badly wrong. You have to believe me that we didn't intend for them to die. I promise we didn't.'

Was she admitting to killing Jayne and Anita?

'What did you do to them exactly?' Whitney asked, scrutinising the woman's facial movements to see if she could spot whether she was telling the truth, even though she knew George would be able to tell her.

'We kidnapped them.'

'Why? What was your intention?' Brian asked.

He couldn't help himself. He had to be a part of it. Whitney was beginning to realise that now. Then again, she couldn't really blame him, when she was younger, she'd been exactly the same.

'We had a static caravan which we kept at a site on the Brampton Road. We tied the girls up and left them there overnight to teach them a lesson for what they'd done. It was to scare them into stopping selling drugs. We knew they could survive that long without food and water. We left the heater on, so they didn't get cold.'

'How did they die?' Whitney asked.

'We don't know. It was such a shock when we went to let them go the next morning and they were both dead. There were no marks on them it was like they died in their sleep.'

'Possibly carbon monoxide poisoning?' George said.

Whitney gave a nod.

'Was it a gas fire that you left on for them?' she asked, remembering the fires they'd had in caravans they'd used in the past.

'Yes. Why?'

'It could very likely be carbon monoxide poisoning from the fire if it was faulty.'

Mrs Robertson covered her mouth with her hand, she aged ten years in front of Whitney's eyes. 'Oh my goodness, that's awful. You don't know how much I've regretted what we did. I hated the girls for stealing Justin from us, but not enough for them to die because I know he was partially to blame.'

'What happened to the caravan?' Whitney asked.

'We advertised it in the local paper and sold it because I couldn't bear to use it again.'

Right. Now where did the inspector fit in to all of this?

'Why did you bury the bodies on Oak Tree Farm?' Whitney asked.

The woman looked at Whitney and then Brian. 'It was out of the way.'

'That's nonsense,' George said in her ear. 'Ask her about the inspector.'

'I understand Malcolm Payne, a retired inspector, is your cousin.'

She glanced up, fear in her eyes. 'How do you know that?'

'It came up during our enquiries.'

'He had nothing to do with it. Nothing. Absolutely nothing.'

'So you didn't choose that location because he went shooting there every week and knew it would be a good, secluded spot?' Whitney asked, locking eyes with her.

'I don't know anything about that. I think maybe I should have a solicitor,' Mrs Robertson said as she slumped into the chair looking exhausted.

'That's a good idea,' Whitney said. 'Peggy Robertson, I'm arresting you on suspicion of the murders of Anita Bailey and Jayne Kennedy. You do not have to say anything, but it may harm your defence if you do not mention when questioned something which you later rely on in court. Anything you do say may be given in evidence. Do you understand?'

'Yes,' Mrs Robertson said, her voice barely above a whisper.

'Interview suspended.' Whitney halted the recording and stood. 'We'll leave you here while we speak to Mr Robertson and then you will be processed.'

'It was an accident,' Mrs Robertson said, hanging her head.

Whitney and Brian left the interview room and met George in the corridor.

'Good job, guv,' Brian said.

'Thanks. Did you believe her story, George?'

'Yes, about it being an accident. No, in respect of the inspector not being involved.'

'My view, too. Brian go back into the interview room

and wait while I arrange for an officer to sit with her. I don't want her calling Payne. Then meet me in Mr Robertson's room.'

'Yes, guv.'

'He did well,' George said, as they went on their way.

'Yes, I'm definitely warming to him and can see he's going to be an asset to the team. He does want to do well, as you said. And don't say *I told you so*,' she added before George had time to speak.

'The thought hadn't entered my head.'

Chapter 31

They waited outside the interview room until Brian arrived and then George left them to observe.

'Sorry to keep you waiting, Mr Robertson,' Whitney said as they walked in and sat down.

'Where have you been? It's been ages,' he growled.

They needed to handle him differently from how they managed his wife.

'We've been talking to Mrs Robertson, and it took longer than expected,' she said.

'I don't see why you couldn't have spoken to us both together.' He gave an exasperated sigh.

'It's police procedure.'

'Where's my wife now? How is she?'

'She's fine. We've left her in the other room and some-one's with her. I'm going to record the interview to save taking notes. Brian, could you do the honours.'

She'd never done this with Matt before, but she wanted to show her appreciation to Brian. George would be proud of her.

'Yes, guv.' Brian turned on the recording equipment.

'Interview on December the twenty-second. Those present: Detective Chief Inspector Walker, Detective Sergeant Chapman. Please state your name,' Brian said to Mr Robertson.

'Kenneth Robertson. But I fail to see why this is all relevant, we're just here to look at some photos.'

'Mr Robertson, now we've spoken to your wife we'd like your side of things,' Whitney said,

'My side of things?' He paled but remained rigid.

'Yes. Do you recognise this man?' She motioned for Brian to put up on the screen the photo of Reg Shaw, again wanting to begin the interview gently.

'No. I've never seen him before in my life,' he said, folding his hands tightly across his chest and giving a sharp nod.

'That's true,' George said.

'What about these two girls?'

Brian put up photos of the victims.

'No. No. Definitely not.'

'Untrue,' George said. 'The way he repeated the words for emphasis, is an indicator.'

'Perhaps you could think again, as according to Mrs Robertson, you *did* know these two. They are Anita Bailey and Jayne Kennedy, the girls who sold drugs to Justin.'

He leant forward with his arms on the table and rested his head in his hands. 'What else did she say?' he muttered, all the fight gone out of his voice.

'She's admitted that you kidnapped the girls, took them to your caravan and left them tied up. When you went back the next day, they'd both died.'

He sat up straight and stared directly at Whitney, a pained expression in his eyes.

'Why did she have to say anything?' He shook his head. 'We could have got through this.'

'Because she's been plagued with guilt since it happened and was glad it finally came out in the open.'

He frowned. 'I didn't know. We made the decision to never speak of it again.'

'Please could you tell me exactly what happened.' She wanted his version to see if it matched his wife's.

'It was an accident. A tragic accident. We intended to teach them a lesson. They shouldn't have been selling drugs to school kids. They should have been held accountable and that's what we wanted to do.'

'Whose idea was it?'

He cleared his throat. 'Mine.'

'I suspect he's covering for his wife, but don't pursue it just yet. Wait until you've got the facts you require, in case he breaks down,' George said.

'How did you manage to persuade the girls to go with you to the caravan?' Whitney asked.

'We parked near their street and when they came home we asked them to get into the car to talk about Justin. They agreed. Once we had them, we took them to the caravan and tied them up.'

'Something's not right,' George said. 'They couldn't have tied them up without a fight. Even though the couple would have been a lot younger they would have needed help. Mrs Robertson is tiny. The other option is that they took the girls separately.'

George was echoing Whitney's thoughts exactly.

'Did you take them to the caravan together or one at a time?' Whitney asked.

'Together. We planned to leave them overnight. We didn't mean for them to die.'

'But they did. What happened to them, do you think?'

'I'm not sure. We went back and found them dead, but there was no apparent cause.'

'Didn't you have any idea of what had happened?'

'It crossed my mind that the gas heater could have been faulty, but I didn't mention it to Peggy because she'd have felt even more guilty as she was the one who turned on the heating for them.'

Was Justin's girlfriend involved? She hadn't thought to ask Mrs Robertson as they hadn't got into the specifics.

'Did Elizabeth, your son's girlfriend, know anything about what you'd done?'

'No. No.' He shook his head vigorously.

'I don't believe him,' George said.

'Are you sure?' Whitney pushed.

'A hundred per cent.'

She'd leave that for now, as it was more important to discuss Payne and how he was involved.

'I'd like to turn to the burying of the bodies. What was your reason for choosing Oak Tree Farm?'

He looked up to the side, his eyes slightly glazed.

'Classic indicator of him making up the story. Watch,' George said.

Whitney noted what the psychologist was referring to and nodded. She waited for him to speak.

'It was an easy place to get to from the caravan and the farm was large, so we didn't think they'd be found.' He exhaled an audible breath.

'What a coincidence that Mrs Robertson's cousin, Inspector Malcolm Payne, went shooting there.'

Panic crossed his face. 'You know about him?'

'That he's related to Mrs Robertson? Yes, we do. I want you to tell me about his involvement. Did he tell you where to bury the bodies?'

'Is that what my wife told you?' His hands were clenched so tightly on the table that his knuckles were white.

'We were hoping you could give us more details,' Whitney said, not answering him. 'After you'd found the girls dead, did you contact Malcolm Payne and ask him what to do?'

His shoulders slumped and he rubbed his brow. 'Peggy did. We didn't know what to do.'

'What did he suggest?'

'I-I can't tell you. It was our fault. You can't blame him.'

'Mr Robertson, it's all going to come out now and it's far better for you if you explain what happened now, rather than in a courtroom.'

'Court … Peggy would never cope. Please, don't make us go to court.'

Whitney winced. This wasn't going to end well, whichever way she looked at it.

'I can't promise what's going to happen, but I do know that we need you to tell us everything you can.'

'Okay,' he said, nodding. 'Malcolm said he knew of a place where we could bury the bodies and they wouldn't be found. But you can't charge him for this, I know what they do to police officers in prison. We can't let that happen. He's old like us.'

'I'm sorry, but that's not up to me. The fact is, he did help you and he also lied during a police investigation to cover it up. Is there anything you've not told us?'

'No, nothing.'

'Thank you. I do have to make this official. Kenneth Robertson, I'm arresting you on suspicion of the murders of Anita Bailey and Jayne Kennedy. You do not have to say anything, but it may harm your defence if you do not mention when questioned something which you later rely on in court. Anything you do say may be given in evidence. Do you understand?'

'Yes,' he said.

'Stay here while we arrange for someone to take you down to the custody sergeant.'

She ended the recording, and they left the room. George joined them in the corridor.

'We've nailed Malcolm Payne, but I think the girlfriend is also involved so we'll see her first. The Robertsons won't be able to alert either of them while they're here in custody. I'll also need to see the super before we speak to him. George, you come with me to see Elizabeth Franklin. Brian, I want you to go upstairs and see if you can trace the caravan.'

Chapter 32

'I need to speak to Claire,' Whitney said, as George pulled out into traffic. 'I want to find out whether it's possible to tell from the remains if it was carbon monoxide poisoning that killed them. I'll put her on speaker so you can hear.' Whitney keyed in Claire's number and put her phone on the dashboard.

George grimaced at the rough way Whitney placed it there, hoping that the leather hadn't been scratched. She kept some leather polish at home, she'd take a look when she got back and buff up any damage.

'Dexter, pathology,' Claire said, when she answered.

'It's Whitney and George. I've got you on speaker. We'd like a quick chat about the girls found on Oak Tree Farm.'

'Have you received the report?'

'Yes, but this is about something else. We suspect they might have died from carbon monoxide poisoning from a faulty gas heater as they'd been tied up and left in a caravan overnight with the heating on. Their bodies were found the next day with no obvious indications of how they had died.'

'Interesting,' Claire said.

'Question. Is it possible that the bones could have absorbed some of the chemical?' George asked.

'No. There are many things you can learn from the bones, but that's not one of them. I can tell if someone had diabetes, or gout, or arthritis, because these can alter the shape of the bones and some of them will become fused. We can sometimes detect whether a person has had cancer because of how the bones were impacted but poisoning from carbon monoxide leaves no such trace. How certain are you of the cause?'

'Not one hundred per cent, but it's the assumption based on what we've learnt so far. We don't have the caravan to confirm this, and even if we did find it, I doubt there'll be any evidence there. Brian's looking into it.'

'Your new boy. How's that working out?'

Whitney frowned in George's direction.

'Good.'

'I didn't scare him off then?'

'Were you worried you had?' George asked, puzzled by Claire's interaction as it wasn't like her to want to chat.

'No. But I'm now trying to be more considerate of others' feelings. Ralph suggested it the other night.'

Whitney mouthed *Wow* in George's direction.

'You can't be too nice, I enjoy watching you subject people to your *treatment*,' Whitney said.

'I'm sure it won't last, I don't suffer fools gladly.'

'That's more like it. By the way, now we've got you on the phone, can you spare the time to come out for a Christmas drink with George and me?'

'When?'

'What about Christmas Eve?'

'No, I've got to endure the departmental drinks party then. Make it in the new year.'

'Okay, I'll be in touch. Thanks for your help.'

'I didn't do anything,' Claire said as she ended the call.

'It's a shame she can't help, but now we have the confessions it should be enough. In my view, we're looking at manslaughter rather than murder, but that's up to the Crown Prosecution Service. It'll be interesting to hear what Elizabeth has to say.' Whitney picked up her phone and returned it to her pocket. 'The three of them were very close, and much of what Mr and Mrs Robertson has told us is vague, especially the way they were able to take the girls.'

'It might be that they had a weapon and that's what *persuaded* the girls to go with them.'

'Yes, but you'd have thought they would have mentioned it. Mind you, they were so upset by it all it could have slipped their minds. I'm sure it will all unfold soon enough. By the way, Clyde wants to meet you sometime.'

'Why?'

'Because you're working with the team. There's no rush. Let's get the case sorted first.'

'Okay. I'll leave it with you.'

After arriving at Glasson Ltd they parked outside and stepped through the doors. The receptionist looked up at them and smiled.

'Have you come back to see Elizabeth?' she asked.

'Yes, we have. Please will you call her.'

After waiting a few minutes, Elizabeth hurried down the corridor towards them.

'Chief Inspector?'

'We would like another word with you,' Whitney said.

Elizabeth led them to a small room that had a circular oak table with four matching chairs. In the centre of the table stood a jug and four glasses.

'We have Mr and Mrs Robertson at the station, and they've been arrested for the kidnap and murder of Anita Bailey and Jayne Kennedy. We know the story and wish to question you on your role,' Whitney said once they were seated.

The woman's face paled and she hugged her chest. 'M-my role?'

'Yes. We also know that Mrs Robertson's cousin, Inspector Malcolm Payne, was involved.'

'What did they say about me?'

'It is our belief that you lured the girls to a place where Mr and Mrs Robertson could kidnap them.'

George nodded her approval at the way Whitney skirted around the question and implied that they knew Elizabeth had been a part of it.

'Um—'

'You might as well tell us the truth because it's going to come out sooner or later. It will be easier on you if you tell us exactly what happened, especially as you were only sixteen at the time and that will be taken into consideration.'

The woman gave a sigh. 'Okay, I'll tell you everything I know. Yes, I did know of their plan to kidnap Anita and Jayne. They asked me if I could arrange for the girls to go to a secluded spot for them.'

'What did you say when they asked? Did you try to stop them?'

'No. I hated Jayne and Anita for what they'd done and thought it would serve them right to pay. It wasn't as if the Robertsons planned to kill them. They wanted to scare them into stopping their drug selling. But … it all went wrong.'

'I'd like you to explain exactly what happened,' Whitney said.

'It wasn't hard to orchestrate. We were in the same class at St Paul's and I told them I wanted to buy some drugs but didn't want to be seen doing so at school. They believed what I said and agreed to meet me at Westfield Park. I chose a time and place when I knew it would be quiet. I let Mr and Mrs Robertson know the details so they could be there, too, and drive them away.'

'How did the Robertsons persuade Jayne and Anita to get into the car?'

'Mr Robertson had a gun and he used that.' George nodded. She'd been right.

'What sort of gun?'

'It was old and rusty. An old pistol, I think. It might have come from the war. You'll have to check with him.'

'What happened when you were all at the meeting point?' Whitney asked.

'Mr Robertson threatened them with it, and they started to cry, begging him not to hurt them. He had no trouble convincing them to get in the car. Mrs Robertson drove, while he sat in the passenger seat, positioned so he could see them. He kept the gun pointing at them for the whole journey.'

'Did they try to escape?'

'No, they were too scared.'

'Where were you?'

'I was seated between them in the back.'

'Did they know you were part of the plan or did they think you'd all been caught?'

'Nothing was said, but I think they might have believed I was caught too. Mr Robertson aimed the gun at all of us. It's possible he didn't want me incriminated once it was all over.'

'But wouldn't they have realised you were in on it when he didn't tie you up?' George asked.

'No, because when we got to the caravan, he put them in separate bedrooms and tied them up with rope. They probably thought I was in the lounge area. He'd gagged them so they couldn't speak to each other. He then locked them in and we all left.'

'Did you go back with them the next day when they found the bodies?' Whitney asked.

'No, I didn't. They told me about it later when I called at their house to see them. It was such a shock. I hated them but didn't want them dead.'

'We believe they died of carbon monoxide poisoning from the gas fire which might have been faulty.'

'I remember Mrs Robertson putting it on for them because she said it got cold at night. I know that sounds strange considering they'd kidnapped them to teach them a lesson. But Mrs Robertson is a very caring woman. If only she hadn't done that, they might still be alive.'

'That's pointless speculation,' George said.

'Did you know about Inspector Payne being involved in the cover-up?'

'Yes, I did, but they didn't tell me exactly what he'd done.'

'Elizabeth Franklin, I'm arresting you on suspicion of being an accessory in the murders of Anita Bailey and Jayne Kennedy. You do not have to say anything, but it may harm your defence if you do not mention when questioned something which you later rely on in court. Anything you do say may be given in evidence. Do you understand?' Whitney asked.

'Yes.'

'You're to accompany us to the station. We won't put you in handcuffs, we will walk out together.'

'But what about my work?'

'Right now, work is the least of your worries,' Whitney said through gritted teeth.

Chapter 33

After Elizabeth Franklin was taken to the custody suite for processing, Whitney turned to George.

'The super asked me to provide her with an update before we do anything about Payne, so I'll go now and ask for permission to bring him in.'

'I'll wait for you in the incident room. I'll catch up on my emails.'

'Good. I want you to observe his interview as it's going to be a tricky one and I'm not sure whether the super will want to be involved, or whether she'll leave us to it. Hopefully the latter.'

Whitney took the lift to Clyde's floor and hurried along the corridor to her office. The door was slightly open, and the super stood by the window staring out. Whitney tapped gently before walking in and standing beside the door.

Clyde turned and smiled. 'Come in.'

'The case is solved, ma'am,' she said, walking further into the office.

'Fill me in, we'll sit around the table.' The super gestured to the meeting table on the far side of her office.

None of the Jamieson stuff of keeping them separated by the desk which Whitney had always felt he'd done to exercise his power over her.

'You're not going to like this, but we have confirmation that Malcolm Payne was definitely involved.'

'We'd prepared ourselves for this, but it's still a difficult situation. Tell me everything.'

'Mr and Mrs Robertson, with the help of their dead son's girlfriend, Elizabeth Franklin, lured the two victims to a quiet place in Westfield Park. Mr Robertson threatened them with a firearm and forced them into the car, which was driven by Mrs Robertson. Franklin remained with them. The victims were taken to a caravan, tied up and left overnight in separate rooms. The intention was to teach them a lesson, but Mrs Robertson was worried about the weather and left the gas fire on for them. When the couple returned the following morning, the girls were dead. Although we can't prove any of this, because it's too long ago and there's no trace of the caravan, we believe the fire was faulty and the girls died of carbon monoxide poisoning.'

'The silent killer,' the super said, nodding. 'No smell to warn them, although if the girls were tied up, they most likely wouldn't have been able to do anything to save themselves. How was Malcolm Payne involved?'

'Mrs Robertson contacted him when they found the bodies and explained the situation, but what happened next is unclear. We're unsure if Payne told them where to bury the bodies, or whether he did it himself. I suspect he might have done it, as he knew the farm well from shooting there regularly. The Robertsons didn't want to incriminate Payne because they were scared of what might happen to him in prison, as he's an ex-police officer, so they're being deliberately vague about it. What I'd like to do next is interview Payne to find out the exact sequence of events and, through questioning, we might be able to ascertain from him his actual role in the proceedings.'

'Okay. Bring him in and let me know how it goes.'

'You mentioned earlier that we should be more informal when bringing him in, so he believes he's helping us. Would you still like it handled in this way?'

'No. Based on the evidence we now have he should be brought in as we would any other suspect.'

'Yes, ma'am. Do you wish to be part of his interview?'

'That's your area of expertise and I won't interfere but keep me up to date at all times.'

'Thank you, ma'am. I'm going to ask Dr Cavendish to observe and I'll interview with DS Chapman.'

'We will need to hold a press conference later. I'll ask Melissa to arrange one. This is excellent work, Whitney. I'm very impressed with the way the investigation has been conducted by you and your team.'

Whitney left the super's office and returned to the incident room, still surprised by the difference in the treatment she was receiving. She'd also noticed that the super had referred to Melissa by name. She doubted Jamieson knew it as he'd only ever referred to the PR department.

She called the team to attention. 'The super has given permission for us to bring in Malcolm Payne for interview. I'm going to ask uniform to do that, so he realises it's official. Dr Cavendish will be watching. Brian, you're with me. We need the truth, but I don't need to tell you that we have to follow regulations to the letter.'

It had to be said, even though she was confident her sergeant wouldn't do anything to jeopardise the investigation.

'Yes, guv. I understand,' Brian said.

'Ellie, contact Anthony Gibson and let him know he can resume work on the development.'

'Yes, guv.'

Whitney went into her office and tried to focus on some of the never-ending admin she had to do, but made little progress. An hour later, she received a call from the front desk to say Malcolm Payne had arrived and he'd been left in one of the interview rooms. She collected George and Brian and the three of them hurried downstairs.

'We'll take this interview steady, remembering he's an old man who broke the law. He most likely realises that he's been caught and will understand what's going to happen. We will respect his position as a retired inspector.'

'Why?' Brian asked. 'I say we go in hard. Even if he has retired, there's still going to be fallout for the force.'

'What he did was put his family first. You should be mindful of the fact it would have been a tough choice for him to make,' George said.

'He covered up two murders and that's not what we do in the job, however much it impacts our family,' Brian said, his lips set in a thin line.

'Two accidental deaths,' Whitney said, correcting him. 'I'm not prepared to discuss this any further. We will be running things my way.'

'Yes, guv.'

After arriving at the interview room, George left them and went into the observation area.

Payne stood when Whitney and Brian went in to speak to him.

'What's going on? I was *escorted* to the station without being told what was happening. I'm not impressed by being treated in this way and demand to know why I'm here.'

'He's going on the offensive to put you off your stride,' George said. 'Impressive, for his age. I suspect he knows full well why he's being interviewed.'

'Please sit down, Malcolm,' Whitney said.

'It's not good enough. I don't expect to be treated like this. I was taken out of my home by officers in uniform for all the people in the village to see. What are they going to think, that the village isn't safe? That they're living near a criminal? I'm very unhappy about my treatment and will be taking it further. I still have plenty of contacts in the force.'

'Sit down,' Whitney repeated, her voice calm but firm. She leant over and started the recording equipment. 'Interview twenty-second of December. Those present: Detective Chief Inspector Walker, Detective Sergeant Chapman. Please state your name,' she said to Payne.

'Malcolm Payne.'

'Mr Payne, we have been interviewing Peggy Robertson, your cousin, regarding the recent discovery of bodies at Oak Tree Farm.'

A raft of expressions crossed his face, from disbelief to resignation and he slumped in his chair, all the fight gone out of him. Whitney was surprised by how quickly it had happened, considering how forceful he'd just been towards them.

'I doubt he'll give you much trouble now he realises what's going to happen,' George said.

Whitney gave a nod. 'Mr and Mrs Robertson are both here at the station and have been charged for their part in what happened to Anita Bailey and Jayne Kennedy.'

'It was an accident,' Payne said, his voice devoid of emotion.

'They've told us the story about the girls dying in the

caravan and we also have Elizabeth Franklin in custody for her part in the proceedings.'

'You have to understand that they were horrified by the girls' deaths. I swear on my life, they didn't intend for it to happen. I admit what they did was stupid, but they were suffering from grief over what had happened to Justin. Had I known in advance what they'd planned to do I would have stopped them, but it wasn't until the girls died that they came to me for help. What else could I do?'

'If it was an accident, and they reached out to you, why didn't you do the right thing and bring them in, instead of concocting a story that Anita and Jayne had run away? You would have saved the girls' parents a great deal of anguish caused by not knowing what had happened.'

'Peggy and Ken had been through enough with Justin dying and I didn't want to make it worse. I'm sorry, I was wrong.'

'How did the girls' bodies get to Oak Tree Farm?'

'What did Peggy and Ken say?'

Surely he wasn't going to lie about it. She gave an exasperated sigh.

'It doesn't matter what they said. I'm asking you. Did you bury the girls, or did you instruct the Robertsons where to take them? We know you were a member of the clay pigeon shooting club that used the farm for practice.'

'You're good,' Payne said, giving a wry smile.

'I have an excellent team. Did you bury the bodies?' Whitney pushed, sure that he was about to confess.

'I had no choice.' He bowed his head.

'There's always a choice,' Brian said, interrupting.

Whitney glared at her sergeant. This wasn't the time for him to go all *holier than thou*. 'You were a serving officer, Malcolm. It could have been dealt with, as you well know.'

'Who are you kidding? They would have been charged

with kidnap and murder because there was no way to prove the deaths were accidental.'

'We believe the girls' deaths were down to a faulty gas fire and that they died of carbon monoxide poisoning. If you'd have investigated before taking the action you did, you would have discovered that and acted correctly.'

'They would still have ended up in prison and I wasn't prepared for that to happen to them. I'd do it again, if the situation arose. If it wasn't for the new housing estate being built no one would've discovered them.'

'Don't you care about the parents of the missing girls?' Whitney asked, surprised he could be so callous.

'There was nothing I could do as I only became involved after the fact.'

'Peggy and Ken tried to hide your involvement, because they thought prison would be bad for you.'

'That sounds like them. They are good people, though I don't expect you to understand.'

Actually, she did. Sort of. But in a similar situation she wouldn't have acted as he had done.

What if it was Tiffany involved?

She pushed that thought to the back of her mind.

'Now you've admitted your involvement, I'd like you to go through everything that happened, chronologically,' Whitney said, choosing to ignore his comment.

'When Peggy phoned me, she was in such a state that I had to help. I couldn't let her suffer more than she had already. Her only child died after taking drugs those girls sold him. They weren't nice girls. Not just because they sold drugs, although that was bad enough. But I later learnt from Elizabeth that they were nasty bullies, and other pupils in their form at school were scared of them. I decided to record them as runaways and that would deal with the situation.'

'What about their parents? For decades they've known nothing of what happened. They held out hope that their daughters were still alive, when in fact they were dead. Didn't you think about them at all?' Whitney drew in a breath, trying to keep it together. Surely, he had some sympathy for the girls' families and the hell they must have gone through for all those years.

'I admit it wasn't an ideal situation and not one I'd have chosen, given the option. There was nothing I could do to bring their daughters back, but it was still possible for me to make life a little easier for Peggy, Ken, and Elizabeth. They deserved that, after all they'd been through.'

On the face of it, his explanation was logical. But as a police officer it was wrong, on so many levels.

'Do you regret what you did?' Whitney asked.

'I don't spend time thinking about it as it would be a pointless exercise when the outcome couldn't be changed.' He shrugged.

Whitney had to force herself to remain calm and not be wound up by this blasé attitude.

'Did you know that Mrs Robertson has been worrying about what happened for all these years? You might not have done her as much of a favour as you believe.'

'I had no idea it was still plaguing her. After everything was over the four of us made a pact to never speak of it again. And I kept to it.'

'Not even when they announced the housing development at Oak Tree Farm?' Brian asked.

'I didn't talk to Peggy and Ken about it, but I was concerned, I must admit.'

'Did you think about going to the burial site and removing the bodies?' Whitney asked.

'I drove out to the farm to take a look, pretending to be walking on the public right of way, but the hedges had already been felled and I couldn't be totally sure where the burial site was. There was nothing I could do but sit back and hope they wouldn't be found. Unfortunately, they were.'

'Does your wife know about any of this?' Whitney asked, curious as to her involvement.

'No.'

'He's lying,' George said in her ear. 'But I wouldn't push it. There's unlikely to be any evidence linking her to the case.'

Whitney agreed, and it was going to be hard enough for his wife as it was.

'Malcolm Payne, I'm arresting you on suspicion of being an accessory in the murders of Anita Bailey and Jayne Kennedy. You do not have to say anything, but it may harm your defence if you do not mention when questioned something which you later rely on in court. Anything you do say may be given in evidence. Do you understand?'

'Yes.'

They escorted him to the custody suite and handed him over to the sergeant to be officially charged.

'What a mess,' Whitney said to Brian. 'The press will have a field day.'

Chapter 34

'Are you ready, Whitney?' Superintendent Clyde asked as she knocked and opened the door to Whitney's office and walked in, looking tall and intimidating in her uniform.

'Yes, ma'am.' Whitney jumped up from behind her desk and attempted to hide her surprise at being collected by her boss.

'This isn't going to be fun because we are accusing one of our own, but it has to be done. It's imperative that we are seen to be squeaky clean at all times.'

She picked up her jacket from the back of the chair and put it on as they left her office, heading down the corridor towards the lift.

'How's the new team panning out now you've solved your first case?' Clyde asked, as she pressed the button to take them to the ground floor.

'Very well, thanks. We had a few hiccups initially, as everyone settled in, but I think it's going to work out well. They all did an excellent job in gathering information required to solve this case.'

'I'm pleased to hear it, especially as I was integral in

putting the team together. I don't want to give anyone cause to think I'd done the wrong thing.'

By *anyone* did she mean Douglas?

They exited the lift and walked down the corridor towards the conference room. Melissa was waiting for them at the entrance.

'Hello, Melissa,' the super said. 'Whitney, as you know, I'm going to do the speaking. You're there for backup if I need it.'

'Yes, ma'am. I understand.'

They entered the room and stood behind the podium. The room was absolutely packed, even more so than usual. Had they got wind of what was about to be announced? It wouldn't surprise her. The media seemed to have a hotline to the station, however hard they tried to keep things quiet.

Melissa called the room to attention, before handing over to Clyde, who stepped up to the podium.

'Thank you all for coming in at such short notice. I'm going to update you on the case concerning the two teenage girls who were found buried on Oak Tree Farm recently, as there have been some substantial developments. Anita Bailey and Jayne Kennedy went missing in 1980 and, at the time, they were recorded as having run away from home. Because of their age it was deemed inappropriate to pursue the matter further. However, following our investigation we have arrested four people in connection with their deaths. At present, we're not releasing the names of those detained, other than to say that one of those charged is a former police officer.'

The noise in the room increased as reporters were muttering to each other. Whitney wasn't looking forward to seeing the headlines later. The police were fair game as far as the media were concerned.

'What's the name of the officer in question?' a woman in the front row called out.

It was only to be expected. They weren't going to let it rest just because the super had said they weren't releasing the names.

'As I've already mentioned,' Clyde said, her voice calm. 'We're not, at this stage, releasing names of the people being charged. We're confident that the case has been solved and we are no longer investigating.'

'Is ex-inspector Malcolm Payne one of those charged?' a reporter in the middle of the room shouted out.

Whitney glanced at the super. Her face gave nothing away, she could just as easily be discussing what she'd had for breakfast instead of police corruption. Whitney could learn a lot from her.

'As I've already stated *twice*, we're not releasing names at this point so it's pointless pursuing this line of questioning.'

'Inspector Payne was in charge of the original investigation, wasn't he?' the reporter continued.

'That is correct,' Clyde confirmed.

'How did the girls die?' the same reporter asked.

Who had primed her? The questions were too direct for it to be otherwise.

'The evidence suggests it was an accident and the girls died from carbon monoxide poisoning after being trapped in a caravan which had a faulty gas fire.'

'What do you mean *trapped*? What are the charges?'

'They include kidnapping and manslaughter.'

'How many police officers have been charged?'

'One. This officer has been charged with being an accessory and conspiring to cover-up an offence. That is all we have for you. Thank you for attending.'

Clyde turned and headed out of the conference room,

followed by Whitney. Once they were out of earshot Whitney turned to her.

'That wasn't too bad, ma'am.'

'No. It could have been a lot worse. Some of the questions were too pointed for them not to have been given the nod.'

'It certainly seemed that way. We'll soon see when the stories are out.'

They took the lift together and Whitney returned to the incident room.

'How was it, guv?' Frank asked as soon as she'd closed the door.

'As to be expected. But now it's over I think we should have an after-work drink to celebrate our first case with the new team.'

'Are the drinks on you, guv?' Frank asked.

'I could've put money on you asking that,' Doug said.

'Your point being?' Frank said.

'I think you know what it is, without me spelling it out.'

'Boys …' Whitney said laughing. They cracked her up. 'Yes, Frank. The first round is on me. We'll try the Railway Tavern as it's close and is bound to end up being our local. I'll give Dr Cavendish a call to see if she'd like to join us.'

She returned to her office to make the call but before she could, her phone rang. She glanced at the screen. It was Martin.

'Hey,' she said.

'Have I caught you at a bad time?'

'No, just the opposite, we've just solved the case we've been working on and have arrested all the relevant people.'

'Does that mean you're free to come out with me tomorrow? I'm passing through and thought we could make a night of it.'

She'd love to see him, but she really wanted to visit her

mum and brother as she'd been neglecting them recently. With Tiffany not being there to share the visiting it was all falling on her shoulders.'

'I'm sorry, I can't make it tomorrow.'

'Are you working over Christmas?'

'I'm off on Christmas Day and Boxing Day, but I've already made arrangements. I'll be seeing my mum and brother on both days.'

'New Year?' he asked, a wistful tone in his voice.

Now she felt mean. 'I'll tell you what, I'll see if I can free up some time and will give you a ring. I promise.'

'Good, because I don't want your present to go to waste.'

'What is it?' Whitney was like a child when it came to Christmas, she loved opening gifts and trying to guess what they were before she pulled the paper off.

'My lips are sealed. You'll have to wait and see.'

'Meanie,' she said, laughing.

'Yes, that's me. I'll speak to you soon.'

She ended the call and smiled to herself. With the exception of Tiffany being so far away, for once she felt her life was heading in the right direction.

Chapter 35

George pulled up outside the Railway Tavern and grimaced. She understood why Whitney had chosen it. It was close to the new station and they'd no doubt be in there often. But even so … She hoped it was more palatable than the previous *plastic* pub they'd frequented, although judging by the exterior she doubted it. Whitney had pulled into the car park at the same time, so she waited for her to get out of her car and they headed for the entrance together.

'I don't think you're going to like it in here,' Whitney said as they pushed open the door and music blared.

'I agree. I doubt we'll be able to hold a conversation, judging by this noise.'

Ross occasionally teased her for being a *fuddy-duddy* because she liked peace and quiet when out for a drink or meal. Not that he wanted it rowdy, but he did have a higher tolerance for noise than she did.

'Don't worry, we won't stay long,' Whitney reassured her.

She didn't want to stand in the way of their celebration, so she'd put up with it for as long as necessary.

The main bar area was huge and square. There were tables with chairs lining the walls and in the rest of the space were tall circular tables for people to stand their drinks on. Most people in there were standing in small groups.

'The team is over there,' George said, after scanning the room and spotting them in the far corner.

They headed over in time to hear Frank regaling everyone with a story.

'And the guv went right up to him. Stood on her tiptoes and gave him what for. It was—'

'It was what?' Whitney said, interrupting, arching an eyebrow.

'I didn't see you there, guv,' the officer said, looking sheepish. 'I was just telling them about the time the bouncer from Scoundrels threatened to punch your lights out, and you made him eat his words. Do you remember the case?'

'I do. The case *and* the idiot bouncer. But before you carry on with the story, which you no doubt will be embellishing, what would you all like to drink?'

Whitney wrote down the drinks order and headed for the bar, leaving George standing on her own. Brian made a beeline for her

'If you're a forensic psychologist, that means you analyse people. Right?' he said.

'That's a very simplistic view of my skills.' Was he engaging in small talk? If so, he could try harder.

'But you do, yeah?'

'Why are you asking?' she said, thinking that there was more to this than she'd first assumed.

'I just wondered how you thought I'd done in the team and wanted to ask if you knew what the guv thinks of me?'

'I can't speak for her, you'll have to ask yourself.'

'No, I'm not going to do that. For such a small person, she's incredibly scary.'

George smiled to herself. 'I wouldn't label her as *scary*. What you've got to remember is that DCI Walker has certain ways of doing things, and she expects loyalty from her team.'

'Do *you* think I'm doing okay?'

'Yes, I think you've performed well up to now, and will improve as you settle into the new role.'

'I'm not planning on staying long.'

'Where are you going?'

'I'm on the up. I'm going to take my Inspectors' exams next year and then I'm going places. I don't intend to hang around Lenchester for long, it's too small and parochial.'

'Are you going to tell DCI Walker your plans?'

'She knows I'm ambitious. Do you think it will go against me?'

'I doubt it will, but you'll have to ask her.'

'I'm not going to rock the boat,' he said.

George was relieved when out of the corner of her eye she saw Whitney on her way back carrying a tray of drinks. When she reached them, she handed them out.

'Here's to our first case as the new team,' Whitney said holding up her glass.

'Three cheers for all of us,' Frank said.

After cheering, Brian left George's side and the team all returned to their conversations.

George turned to Whitney. 'What's going to happen with Reg Shaw. Are you going to assist with his parole when it comes up?'

'I'll wait to see if I'm approached. The information he

provided wasn't crucial, but it did help in a roundabout way. Do you fancy going back to mine with a takeaway after here?'

'Yes, that would be nice.'

'We can sit quietly and have a chat.'

'Unlike here, it's so loud.' George shook her head.

'We'll get used to it. I saw you were talking to Brian, what was he saying?'

'He wanted to know what you thought of him,' she said quietly.

'Seriously?'

'Yes, seriously,' she said.

'You surprise me. What else did he say?'

'He told me his plans for his career.'

'He's already intimated that he's not planning on staying here long.'

'I'm sure he won't, but until he goes, I'm sure you'll get on with him just fine.'

'I still prefer the old team.'

'Well, you can't have the old team so it's pointless talking about it.'

'Yes, I know what you're saying.' Whitney finished her drink and put her glass on the table. 'Come on then, are you ready?'

They left the pub and stopped to pick up a pizza. They both drew up at Whitney's house together, and as George got out of her car, she noticed the lights were on.

'I'm sure I didn't leave them on when I left this morning,' Whitney said, as she walked over to her.

'Perhaps you did without realising.'

Knowing how slapdash Whitney could be at home, it wouldn't have surprised her.

They walked up the path and Whitney used her key to open the door. In the hallway stood two suitcases.

'Tiffany's here,' Whitney shouted. 'That's her suitcase. Tiffany,' she called out.

'In the kitchen,' the girl shouted back.

Whitney ran into the kitchen with George following. Tiffany was sitting at the table next to a young man with long, curly blond hair which came to his shoulders. She jumped up and hugged her mum.

'Hello, Mum,' the young woman said between tears and laughter.

'You're home,' Whitney said as she wiped away her own tears. 'Why didn't you tell me?'

'I wanted it to be a surprise,' Tiffany said grinning.

'Hello,' George said, stepping forward so the young girl could see her.

'George …' Tiffany rushed over and gave her a hug.

She froze. Hugs were strange.

'It's good to see you.'

'Mum. George. I want to introduce you to Lachlan. We met in Australia.'

Whitney and George exchanged a glance. Was he her boyfriend?

'Pleased to meet you, Lachlan,' George said holding out her hand.

'Good to meet you, too,' he replied in a broad Australian accent.

'I have pizza we can share,' Whitney said. 'I'll open up a bottle of wine to celebrate.'

Tiffany looked at Lachlan, a guarded expression on her face. 'Before we do anything, I've got something to tell you.'

'You're not going back to Australia, are you? I thought you were back to stay, I—'

'Mum. Stop. I'm back to stay. We both are.'

'Both?' Whitney frowned.

'I have a British passport because my mum is from Scotland,' Lachlan said.

'But that's not what I want to tell you,' Tiffany said.

'You're not sick, are you?' Whitney said, feeling Tiffany's forehead.

'No. I'm not sick. It's—'

'Tiffany, just tell me,' Whitney begged.

'I'm trying but you keep interrupting with your questions,' she said, tapping her foot impatiently.

'You know what I'm like. I promise I won't speak again until I've heard your news.' Whitney stood next to her daughter, her body rigid.

Tiffany glanced at Lachlan, and bit down on her bottom lip.

What on earth was it?

'I'm pregnant.'

'What?' Whitney spluttered.

'Yes. You're going to be a granny.'

Book 10 - Whitney and George return in ***Kill Shot*** when they investigate the shooting dead of Lenchester's most famous sportsman. An investigation which has far-reaching, international ramifications.

Tap here to buy

GET ANOTHER BOOK FOR FREE!

To instantly receive the free novella, ***The Night Shift***, featuring Whitney when she was a Detective Sergeant, ten years ago, sign up for Sally Rigby's free author newsletter at www.sallyrigby.com

Read more about Cavendish & Walker

DEADLY GAMES - Cavendish & Walker Book 1

A killer is playing cat and mouse……. and winning.

DCI Whitney Walker wants to save her career. Forensic psychologist, Dr Georgina Cavendish, wants to avenge the death of her student.

Sparks fly when real world policing meets academic theory, and it's not a pretty sight.

When two more bodies are discovered, Walker and Cavendish form an uneasy alliance. But are they in time to save the next victim?

Deadly Games is the first book in the Cavendish and Walker crime fiction series. If you like serial killer thrillers and psychological intrigue, then you'll love Sally Rigby's page-turning book.

Pick up *Deadly Games* today to read Cavendish & Walker's first case.

FATAL JUSTICE - Cavendish & Walker Book 2

A vigilante's on the loose, dishing out their kind of justice…

A string of mutilated bodies sees Detective Chief Inspector Whitney Walker back in action. But when she discovers the victims have all been grooming young girls, she fears a vigilante is on the loose. And while she understands the motive, no one is above the law.

Once again, she turns to forensic psychologist, Dr Georgina Cavendish, to unravel the cryptic clues. But will they be able to save the next victim from a gruesome death?

Fatal Justice is the second book in the Cavendish & Walker crime fiction series. If you like your mysteries dark, and with a twist, pick up a copy of Sally Rigby's book today.

~

DEATH TRACK - Cavendish & Walker Book 3

Catch the train if you dare...

After a teenage boy is found dead on a Lenchester train, Detective Chief Inspector Whitney Walker believes they're being targeted by the notorious Carriage Killer, who chooses a local rail network, commits four murders, and moves on.

Against her wishes, Walker's boss brings in officers from another force to help the investigation and prevent more deaths, but she's forced to defend her team against this outside interference.

Forensic psychologist, Dr Georgina Cavendish, is by her side in an attempt to bring to an end this killing spree. But how can they get into the mind of a killer who has already killed twelve times in two years without leaving a single clue behind?

For fans of Rachel Abbott, L J Ross and Angela Marsons, *Death Track* is the third in the Cavendish & Walker series. A gripping serial killer thriller that will have you hooked.

LETHAL SECRET - Cavendish & Walker Book 4

Someone has a secret. A secret worth killing for....

When a series of suicides, linked to the Wellness Spirit Centre, turn out to be murder, it brings together DCI Whitney Walker and forensic psychologist Dr Georgina Cavendish for another investigation. But as they delve deeper, they come across a tangle of secrets and the very real risk that the killer will strike again.

As the clock ticks down, the only way forward is to infiltrate the centre. But the outcome is disastrous, in more ways than one.

For fans of Angela Marsons, Rachel Abbott and M A Comley, *Lethal Secret* is the fourth book in the Cavendish & Walker crime fiction series.

LAST BREATH - Cavendish & Walker Book 5

Has the Lenchester Strangler returned?

When a murderer leaves a familiar pink scarf as his calling card, Detective Chief Inspector Whitney Walker is forced to dig into a cold case, not sure if she's looking for a killer or a copycat.

With a growing pile of bodies, and no clues, she turns to forensic psychologist, Dr Georgina Cavendish, despite their relationship being at an all-time low.

Can they overcome the bad blood between them to solve the

unsolvable?

For fans of Rachel Abbott, Angela Marsons and M A Comley, *Last Breath* is the fifth book in the Cavendish & Walker crime fiction series.

FINAL VERDICT - Cavendish & Walker Book 6

The judge has spoken......everyone must die.

When a killer starts murdering lawyers in a prestigious law firm, and every lead takes them to a dead end, DCI Whitney Walker finds herself grappling for a motive.

What links these deaths, and why use a lethal injection?

Alongside forensic psychologist, Dr Georgina Cavendish, they close in on the killer, while all the time trying to not let their personal lives get in the way of the investigation.

For fans of Rachel Abbott, Mark Dawson and M A Comley, Final Verdict is the sixth in the Cavendish & Walker series. A fast paced murder mystery which will keep you guessing.

RITUAL DEMISE - Cavendish & Walker Book 7

Someone is watching.... No one is safe

The once tranquil woods in a picturesque part of Lenchester have become the bloody stage to a series of ritualistic murders. With no suspects, Detective Chief Inspector Whitney Walker is once again forced to call on the services of forensic psychologist Dr Georgina Cavendish.

But this murderer isn't like any they've faced before. The murders are highly elaborate, but different in their own way and, with the clock ticking, they need to get inside the killer's head before it's too late.

For fans of Angela Marsons, Rachel Abbott and L J Ross. Ritual Demise is the seventh book in the Cavendish & Walker crime fiction series.

MORTAL REMAINS - Cavendish & Walker Book 8

Someone's playing with fire…. There's no escape.

A serial arsonist is on the loose and as the death toll continues to mount DCI Whitney Walker calls on forensic psychologist Dr Georgina Cavendish for help.

But Lenchester isn't the only thing burning. There are monumental changes taking place within the police force and there's a chance Whitney might lose the job she loves. She has to find the killer before that happens. Before any more lives are lost.

Mortal Remains is the eighth book in the acclaimed Cavendish & Walker series. Perfect for fans of Angela Marsons, Rachel Abbot and L J Ross.

SILENT GRAVES - Cavendish & Walker Book 9

Nothing remains buried forever…

When the bodies of two teenage girls are discovered on a building site, DCI Whitney Walker knows she's on the hunt for a killer. The problem is the murders happened in 1980 and this is her first case with the new team. What makes it even tougher is that with budgetary restrictions in place, she only has two weeks to solve it.

Once again, she enlists the help of forensic psychologist Dr Georgina Cavendish, but as she digs deeper into the past, she uncovers hidden truths that reverberate through the decades and into the present.

Silent Graves is the ninth book in the acclaimed Cavendish & Walker series. Perfect for fans of L J Ross, J M Dalgleish and Rachel Abbott.

~

KILL SHOT - Cavendish & Walker Book 10

The game is over.....there's nowhere to hide.

When Lenchester's most famous sportsman is shot dead, DCI Whitney Walker and her team are thrown into the world of snooker.

She calls on forensic psychologist Dr Georgina Cavendish to assist, but the investigation takes them in a direction which has far-reaching, international ramifications.

Much to Whitney's annoyance, an officer from one of the Met's special squads is sent to assist.

But as everyone knows...three's a crowd.

Kill Shot is the tenth book in the acclaimed Cavendish & Walker series. Perfect for fans of Simon McCleave, J M Dalgleish, J R Ellis and Faith Martin.

Acknowledgments

My thanks, as always, go to the best critique partners and friends anyone could have. Amanda Ashby and Christina Phillips, without you none of this would have been possible.

Thanks also to Kate Noble, my advanced readers, my fantastic editor Emma Mitchell, and my awesome cover designer, Stuart Bache (for producing one of my favourite covers). I'm so lucky to have you on my team.

To my family, thanks for always being in my corner. I really appreciate all of your support.

About the Author

Sally Rigby was born in Northampton, in the UK. She has always had the travel bug, and after living in both Manchester and London, eventually moved overseas. From 2001 she has lived with her family in New Zealand, which she considers to be the most beautiful place in the world. During this time she also lived for five years in Australia.

Sally has always loved crime fiction books, films and TV programmes, and has a particular fascination with the psychology of serial killers.

Sally loves to hear from her readers, so do feel free to get in touch via her website www.sallyrigby.com

Made in the USA
Coppell, TX
02 November 2022

85638867R00162